Praise for

Campus Cravings

The *Campus Cravings* series by Carol Lynne is one of my all-time favourite homoerotic romance series... I LOVED LOVED LOVED this book! I highly recommend reading the books in series order. ~ *Night Owl Romance*

I, for one, have been waiting for Ms. Lynne to release the new addition to the *Campus Cravings* series! It was beautiful to experience as they rekindled their relationship, but will they get a second chance at love? ~ *Fallen Angel Reviews*

I liked this book and the return to the campus...a quick read with a good flow and characterisation...I can't wait for the next release... ~ *Literary Nymphs Reviews*

Total-E-Bound Publishing books by Carol Lynne:

Campus Cravings Volume One: On the Field
Coach
Side-Lined
Sacking the Quarterback

Campus Cravings Volume Two: Off the Field
Off Season
Forbidden Freshman

Campus Cravings Volume Three: Back on Campus
Broken Pottery
In Bear's Bed

Campus Cravings Volume Four: Dorm Life
Office Advances
A Biker's Vow

Campus Cravings Volume Five: BK House
Hershie's Kiss
Theron's Return

Live for Today

Good-Time Boys
Sonny's Salvation
Garron's Gift
Rawley's Redemption
Twin Temptations

Cattle Valley Volume One
All Play & No Work
Cattle Valley Mistletoe

Cattle Valley Volume Two
Sweet Topping
Rough Ride

Cattle Valley Volume Three
Physical Therapy
Out of the Shadow

Cattle Valley Volume Four
Bad Boy Cowboy
The Sound of White

CAMPUS CRAVINGS
Volume Six

Incoming Freshman

A Lesson Learned

CAROL LYNNE

Campus Cravings Volume Six
ISBN # 978-0-85715-773-7
©Copyright Carol Lynne 2011
Cover Art by Posh Gosh ©Copyright August 2011
Interior text design by Claire Siemaszkiewicz
Total-E-Bound Publishing

Published in 2012 by Total-E-Bound Publishing, Think Tank, Ruston Way, Lincoln, LN6 7FL, United Kingdom.

INCOMING
FRESHMAN

Dedication

It was nice to revisit my old friends on campus, but it was even nicer to meet the new ones. I'm looking forward to the next chapter in these men's lives.

Chapter One

North Central Idaho University football coach Chet Sloan dropped the sheet of paper like it was on fire. "No," he whispered, tapping his fingers on the table. He felt like every inappropriate fantasy was coming back to haunt him.

Swallowing around the lump in his throat, Chet picked up the phone and called Justin Nelson.

"Nelson," Justin answered.

"Hey, Coach, it's Chet. Just read the note you left."

"Great news, huh? I couldn't believe it when Sikes called and said he wanted to transfer to NCIU. Do you have any idea how many colleges would love to get their hands on him?"

"Why'd he call you instead of me?" Chet asked. Although Justin was once the head coach at NCIU, he'd taken a position as a junior high school coach after his stroke two years earlier. Unfortunately Chet was beginning to regret his decision to ask Justin to recruit for him in the off-season. Justin had already made a huge impact on the quality of players agreeing to play at NCIU, but the newest transfer could spell big trouble for Chet.

"I guess because my name's listed on the website for recruiting. Hell, I didn't even have to talk the kid into it. He asked me to check on credit transfers from the University of Arizona and the possibility of a scholarship and that was that. I thought you'd be thrilled. Bobby Ray Sikes is the best running back in college football. It's an absolute miracle he wants to transfer here."

"Not such a miracle. I recruited him out of high school for UA," Chet informed his former boss.

"So you know him? That's fantastic. He must think a lot of you to transfer before his senior year. If I'd have known, I would've transferred the call instead of just leaving you the note."

Chet leaned back in his chair and rubbed his forehead. The older he got, the more forehead there was for him to rub. It was all his father's fault he was starting to lose his hair at the age of thirty-two.

"Why do I get the feeling you're less than happy about this?" Justin asked.

Chet dropped his hand. He knew he should tell Justin the truth, but confessing to your mentor that you'd fallen for an eighteen-year-old while recruiting him was just plain embarrassing. It was downright perverse that he'd begun to have dreams about Bobby Ray before the boy had even graduated high school. To top off Chet's shame, Bobby's family had invited him into their home on many occasions, treating him more like family than anyone ever had.

"What aren't you telling me?" Justin prompted.

"There's history there. He didn't take it well when he heard I was leaving UA. Guess I'm not sure how

I'll handle seeing him again, but I know it's good for the school."

"It's great for the school, but if you don't think you can coach him, maybe we need to discuss it before he makes the move."

Chet had no doubt he could coach Bobby. Although he'd run to Idaho to put distance between them, he'd still kept close tabs on Bobby's career. Bobby was one of those players meant for greatness. Chet had seen it years earlier when Bobby's high school football coach had sent him videos of the young man as a freshman.

He'd made his first visit to the family when Bobby was a junior. Sitting in the stands for the first time watching Bobby Ray Sikes play, Chet's skin had broken out in gooseflesh. At the time it was the talent he'd yearned to get his hands on and not the young man's body, but things had changed by the time Bobby turned eighteen. For some reason that was the magic number as far as Chet's libido was concerned. It was soon after Bobby signed the letter of intent to play for the UA that Chet knew he was in trouble.

Afraid that the NCIU would replace him as head coach in favour of getting a big name player like Bobby Ray, Chet had little choice. "I can coach him. As a matter-of-fact, I've got a few ideas of how to improve his game."

Justin chuckled. "I didn't think it was possible to improve his game. The kid's by far the best college player I've ever seen."

"Yeah," Chet agreed. "When's he due to arrive?"

"Thursday." Justin cleared his throat. "He's...umm...requested placement at BK House."

"Ahh, shit." Chet thought of the ramifications of Bobby's decision. Although Chet knew Bobby's secret, the rest of the world didn't. Living in the privately owned dormitory for gay college students would be headline news. "Did you try to talk him out of it?"

"Of course I did, but he's adamant that he wants to set things right before his career goes any further."

"What career? If he goes through with this, it could very well be career suicide." Chet knew he had to talk Bobby out of making the biggest mistake of his life. "You got a number where I can reach him?"

"Yeah." Justin read off a number Chet didn't recognise.

"Is that a cell?" Chet asked.

"No. He's home with his mom right now, but if you're hoping to reach him, you'd better do it now. I think he's planning to head this way later today."

Of course he'd be with Ellen. Along with his guilt over the way he'd handled things with Bobby, Chet carried the knowledge that he hadn't had the balls to attend Martin's funeral the previous year. Sure he'd sent a large bouquet of flowers to the funeral home, but he hadn't attended or sent a personal note. Chet had known it was the coward's way, but it was the only way he could guarantee Bobby's future success.

"Does Ellen know where her son plans to live?" Chet doubted it.

"No idea. I mean she knows where he's moving, but whether or not she knows what BK House is I don't have a clue."

"Okay." Chet had a sinking feeling about the call he was about to make. "Let me talk to him and let you know how it goes."

"I'll be here all afternoon. Unlike you, junior high coaches don't have to start school before the term begins."

"Don't rub it in," Chet said before ending the call. He stared at the name scratched onto the piece of paper. It hadn't taken long after he'd run to Idaho to start thinking of Bobby Ray as just Bobby, the name the young man had asked to be called. At the time he'd refused, knowing it would blur the lines between coach and...something more. A quick glance at the clock and he decided to go have some lunch before talking to Bobby. Sure he was putting off the conversation, but, hell, he'd put it off for three years, what was another hour?

* * * *

Bobby was winding down from his afternoon exercises when the phone rang. "I'll get it," he told his mom. "Hello?"

"Bobby Ray?"

From his reclined position on the sofa, Bobby bolted upright. "Chet?"

There was a moment of silence before Chet spoke again. "Justin Nelson just told me you're interested in transferring to Idaho."

Bobby detected unease in Chet's normally smooth voice. "It's a done deal. The only question is whether or not you'll let me play ball?"

"We both know that's not an option. The college would have my head if I refused to let you play, Bobby Ray, and you know it."

It wasn't the response Bobby had hoped for. Maybe he'd been naïve to think Chet would welcome him now that he was a few years older. "I've asked you more than once to please call me Bobby."

"I know," Chet replied. "But Bobby Ray helps me to remember who you are."

Bobby rolled his eyes. Growing up with two first names had been okay. Actually, he still enjoyed hearing all three names when he ran out onto the football field, but hearing the names from Chet didn't feel right, and while others continued to call him Bobby Ray, he couldn't imagine a lover calling him that. "You're not planning to quit before I get there this time, are you?"

Chet sighed into the phone. "We both know why I left AU."

"I'm not eighteen anymore," Bobby mumbled.

"I understand that, but you're a shoe-in for a first round draft pick. Actually, that's one of the reasons I called. I think you should reconsider moving into BK House."

"Why, because you think it'll ruin my career? I've already been over all this with Coach Nelson and my mom. I've lived a lie for long enough. There's no way I'm going to spend the rest of my life pretending to be something I'm not."

"No one's asking you to, but throwing your sexuality at the press by living in BK House is career suicide." Chet went quiet for just a moment. "Wait a minute. Your mom knows?"

"Yeah and she's okay with it, so don't bring her into it."

"Does she know about...?"

Bobby heard the shame in Chet's voice. No, he wasn't about to travel down that road over the phone. This was his decision, and no one was going to talk him out of it. "Dammit, Chet. Listen to what I'm telling you. I won't live in one of the campus dorms. I've just spent three years trying to live under the watchful eyes of football fans, and I'm sick of it."

"What if I can find you an alternative? Would you at least consider it?"

Bobby didn't understand why it was so important to Chet where he lived, as long as it wasn't with him. "I can't afford to live off campus. Unless, of course, you're offering up your place?" He knew it was just wishful thinking and all that.

"No, but I may be able to find you a room with a like-minded individual or two. Let me work on it, and I'll call you back. What time are you leaving today?"

"I'm not. I'm going with Mom to a doctor's appointment."

"Nothing serious, I hope."

Bobby scrambled for something to say. "Not really, but after what happened to Dad...well, I'd just feel better leaving knowing she's okay." His dad's death the previous year had been the hardest thing he'd ever had to deal with, Chet's abandonment being the second, and the realisation that he'd probably never make it to pro ball being the third. He'd somehow managed to come to grips with the second and third items, but his feelings for Chet hadn't dissipated in the least. He still wanted the man more than he'd ever wanted anything in his life.

"Okay. I'll try to call back before you leave. Do you have a cell phone in case I miss you?"

Bobby glanced at the cell phone sitting on the coffee table. "Yeah, but it's one of those puny prepaid kind. Mom bought it for the trip out. She hates the thought of me driving that far by myself, but she's just not up to the trip."

"I understand. Here, let me give you my number in case you run into any problems on the way," Chet began.

"Don't need it." Bobby rattled off Chet's old cell number. "That one still good?"

There was a moment of silence. "Yes. I can't believe you still remember it."

"I remember everything," Bobby said before hanging up.

The memories of the best night of his life thrust him back into the past. It had been a month after his high school graduation. He'd travelled to Arizona from Arkansas to look at the AU campus for the first time and get expert coaching on what he needed to work on over the summer. The trip had meant even more to Bobby because the plane ticket had been a graduation present from his mom and dad.

Bobby Ray stepped off the plane and made his way with the other passengers to the baggage claim area. He hadn't bothered checking his duffle bag, but had arranged to meet Coach Sloan there.

Rounding the corner, Bobby Ray smiled when he spotted the handsome man. "Hey." He was happily surprised when his soon-to-be coach pulled him in for a quick hug. Bobby Ray's eyes drifted shut at the contact, but before he could sink deeper into Chet's touch, his coach pulled back.

"Is that all you brought?" Chet asked, pointing at Bobby Ray's duffle.

"Yeah. Mom found out it costs twenty-five bucks to check one and repacked for me." Bobby Ray glanced around at the passengers huddled around the luggage carousel. Fools, he thought.

"Well, in that case, I'm parked out this way," Chet said, leading the way towards one of the big doors. "How was your flight?"

"Okay. Long. They gave me a seat in one of the exit rows, though, so that helped." Bobby Ray purposely let Chet walk a few paces in front of him in an effort to study the muscled butt he'd fantasised a lot about lately. He'd known for years

that his sexual preferences weren't in line with the other guys in his high school, so he'd always used his focus on football as an excuse to get out of dating girls. Now that he was about to embark on a different chapter in his life, he wanted to drop some of his walls and let his true personality shine through.

When Chet suddenly stopped walking, Bobby Ray was so busy staring at his ass he didn't have time to stop his forward momentum. "Ooomph," he grunted, running into Chet's chest.

"You okay?" Chet asked, setting a hand on Bobby Ray's shoulder.

Bobby Ray froze, wondering if his coach had caught him staring. "Yeah. Just clumsy today, I guess."

Chet gave Bobby Ray's shoulder a slight squeeze before releasing him. "This is it," he gestured towards a maroon Toyota Highlander. He took Bobby Ray's bag and tossed it into the backseat.

Buckling his seatbelt, Bobby Ray thought about the days ahead. He would only be in town for two more days and wanted to try and bridge the gap between friends and lovers. Naïve, maybe, but he had a goal and he wasn't known for doing anything half-assed.

For the next ten days Bobby Ray hung on every word Chet uttered. He'd never met a man who was so much fun while being so down to earth. There wasn't a single thing about Chet that Bobby Ray didn't find fascinating. Heck the man's hands doing something as simple as turning the knob on the radio turned Bobby on.

It seemed that every night of Bobby Ray's stay Chet had something special planned. So he was more than happy when Chet announced they were due for a break on Bobby Ray's last night in town. His plan was to grill steaks and swim, maybe watch a movie before turning in early. Bobby Ray was secretly thrilled they'd be staying at Chet's small adobe-style house.

Bobby Ray followed Chet outside to the small backyard. "I love it here but it's so different." The small backyard was all cement and pool with a wide cloth awning that shaded the majority of the patio. He was used to his portion of Arkansas where the landscape was green and lush.

Chet lit the gas grill and stepped back. "Yeah, I imagine it'll take some getting used to, but you'll fit in soon enough." Chet glanced at Bobby Ray and once again their eyes met in a heated stare for several moments before Chet turned away. "Why don't you go ahead and change into your swimsuit."

"I didn't bring one." At home he usually swam in the pond behind their house in a ratty pair of cut-off jeans. There was no way he was bringing those gross things for a weekend in the city.

"I've got a bunch of trunks in my bottom dresser drawer. Feel free to find a pair that fit." Chet placed two foil wrapped potatoes on the grill.

"Aren't you going to change?" Bobby Ray couldn't wait to see Chet in a pair of trunks. His mouth began to water just thinking about it.

"Yeah, once you get changed, I'll sneak in and grab a pair." Chet didn't turn to face Bobby Ray although there was no longer a reason to stare at the closed grill.

As Bobby Ray made his way to Chet's bedroom, he began to wonder whether the look they'd exchanged had affected Chet as much as it had him. The thought sent another wave of arousal through him.

He stepped foot inside Chet's room and inhaled deeply. The entire bedroom smelt of the citrus cologne Chet seemed to favour. It was a man's scent, something Bobby Ray had only dreamed of. Pulling open the bottom drawer, Bobby Ray was surprised by how many pairs of swim trunks Chet owned. He figured it must be usual for someone who had a pool in their backyard.

With everything from long board shorts to tiny Speedos, Chet had a wide selection. Bobby Ray pulled out a pair of bright red Speedos and held them up. He doubted he'd ever seen anything so damn tiny. Hell, even Bobby Ray's underwear was bigger than the scrap of red fabric. No doubt the tight fitting suit would show every bump and hair hidden beneath it.

Grinning like a fool, Bobby Ray tucked the suit under his arm and closed the drawer. He was tempted to snoop, but he didn't want to get caught and have it ruin everything. "All done," he called out before slipping into the guestroom.

Bobby Ray shucked his clothing and pulled on the tight Speedo. A quick look in the mirror almost had him backing out. Never had he exposed himself so fully outside a locker room shower.

He reached down and readjusted his balls. Satisfied, Bobby Ray strolled out to the patio, praying he wasn't about to make a fool of himself.

"Did you find...?" Chet's jaw dropped at his first look at Bobby Ray. "Oh."

Bobby Ray watched Chet's Adam's apple bob several times as his gaze worked its way down Bobby Ray's body. "Hope you don't mind," Bobby Ray said, trying to break the tension between them. "I've always wondered what something like this would feel like."

Chet's eyes remained riveted to Bobby Ray's growing cock for several seconds too long. Gotcha, Bobby Ray thought.

"I'm sorry," Chet mumbled, turning to dart into the house.

With a smile on his face, Bobby Ray followed his coach inside. He caught up with Chet in the hallway and reached out to place a hand on the man's broad back. "There's no reason to apologise. I like the way I feel when you look at me."

Chet finally turned to face Bobby Ray, resting his back against the doorframe. "You shouldn't like it. It's wrong, Bobby Ray."

For the first time in his life, Bobby Ray hated the name he'd been strapped with as an infant. He wanted Chet to see him as a man, not a teenager from a hick town, not a football player. Bobby stepped closer until his body barely brushed Chet's. "Call me Bobby, please. I'm eighteen. Old enough to know what I want and legal enough to get it." Although he'd never kissed a man in passion, Bobby's mouth slowly descended on Chet's.

The first touch of Chet's lips sent Bobby's body into overdrive. He pressed further against the muscled body in front of him and opened his mouth. He wasn't stupid enough to think he could pull a kiss off unless he was shown the proper way, so Bobby parted his lips and prayed Chet would take advantage.

With a loud groan, Chet's tongue thrust into his mouth as his fingers burrowed in Bobby's thick hair. Chet's free hand wrapped around Bobby's waist and pulled their bodies together.

Bobby thrilled at the feel of Chet's erection pressing against him. It was his first exploration and he couldn't imagine a better teacher. He moved from side to side as Chet's continued to explore his mouth. The rub of his cock against Chet's was more than he ever thought it would be.

When Chet's hand slipped down to run the length of Bobby's crack through the Speedo, Bobby lost it. His body bucked against Chet's as he broke the kiss to cry out. "Coach!"

The moment the word escaped Bobby's mouth, Chet's body went rigid. He pushed Bobby back and escaped into his room and slammed the door.

As relaxed as he ever had been, Bobby slumped against the bedroom door. "Chet? Did I do something wrong?" He looked down at the mess he'd made of Chet's swim trunks.

He tried the doorknob to no avail. "Please talk to me," he begged.

"You'd better go change into your street clothes, Bobby Ray," Chet eventually said through the closed door.

"Why?" Bobby pressed his palm against the door.

"I'm taking you to the airport."

Bobby was left dumbfounded. Was he being thrown out? Had he made that big a fool of himself that Chet didn't even want him to stay until morning? A thought suddenly occurred to him. He knows I'm a virgin.

Embarrassed, Bobby fled to the guestroom. While he dressed and gathered his clothes, he vowed to learn everything he could about pleasing a lover before the semester started. Maybe then Chet would see him as Bobby and not Bobby Ray.

"You about ready?" Ellen asked, walking into the living room.

Bobby started, coming out of his memory. He was glad he'd grabbed one of the sofa pillows to rest over his hard cock. "In a minute. Do you have the MRI film Dr Petterman gave you?"

"Shoot. I knew I was forgetting something." Ellen hurried back into the kitchen.

Bobby used the excuse to toss the pillow to the couch and disappear into his room. Once behind his closed door, all it took was the memory of Chet's desertion to ease the erection trapped behind his fly.

The memory of showing up on the Arizona campus — only to find out Chet had quit and taken a job in Idaho had driven him that first year. He'd put every ounce of pain into training and performing on the field in an attempt to somehow show Chet what he'd missed out on by leaving like he had. When not one note came from Chet on Bobby being named to the All-American team his freshman year he was more determined than ever.

Bobby changed into a pair of jeans. He couldn't help but wonder whether he was making a huge mistake by transferring to Idaho in an attempt to get closer to Chet. Maybe the kiss they'd shared years earlier hadn't meant anything to Chet.

The thought that he was just another recruit in Chet's eyes caused an ache in Bobby's chest. *No*, he told himself. It wasn't nonchalance he'd seen in Chet's expression that night. Believing it was his lack of experience that had turned Chet away, Bobby had spent the first two-years indulging in secret dates with like-minded men in Arizona.

When the last man he'd spent time with had threatened to 'out' him to the press if he didn't continue their relationship, Bobby had known his sexual education had to come to an end. With his father still alive and professional scouts attending every game, the last thing he had needed was to screw up his future for a night of fucking. He'd realised he could bed half the gay men in Arizona and none of them would ever compare to that one moment with Chet.

After the sudden death of his dad and the injury he'd sustained in the off-season, Bobby had begun laying the groundwork to transfer to Idaho. He'd even spoken to his mother about his feelings for Chet. In a surprise move, Ellen had wrapped her arms around Bobby and praised him for finally being honest with her.

It seemed his mom had known for years that Bobby wasn't like most of the boys he'd grown up with. When Chet had come into the picture, she confessed she'd witnessed the mutual attraction, but according to her, she'd seen something more in Chet's eyes on the night of Bobby's graduation.

Bobby prayed that whatever his mom had seen in Chet's eyes was still there when he got to Idaho.

Chapter Two

Chet parked in front of BK House and turned off the engine. He didn't blame Bobby for wanting to move into the homey building. Unlike most dormitories on the NCIU campus, BK House was definitely one of a kind. From the front, it looked like a typical family home. It wasn't until you walked to the back that the full extent of what the rooms offered was revealed.

Instead of barging in, Chet opted to ring the doorbell. Although there were a few students who stayed at BK over the summer break, it was still the full-time home of the three men who oversaw the running of the house. He'd become friendly with Charlie and Jack, but hadn't met the newest addition to BK.

The front door opened to a nude expansive chest. Chet's gaze slowly worked its way up to the face attached to such a gorgeous body. *Oh, damn.* Amused emerald green eyes met Chet's.

"May I help you?"

Chet untwisted his tongue and held out his hand. "I'm Chet Sloan, football coach here at the university. You must be Lockwood."

"Yes, but please call me Locky," he said and shook Chet's hand. Locky gestured towards his bare chest, glistening with sweat. "Not the best first impression, I guess, but the air conditioning's acting up." He took a step back and ushered Chet into the house.

The moment Chet stepped foot in the foyer, he was met with a blast of warm air. "Whoo, you weren't kiddin'. How long's it been this way?"

"Just today. Demitri has someone coming out tomorrow to check it out. Charlie said the system isn't used often, but with these unseasonably hot temperatures we've been running it almost every day." Locky shrugged. "We've decided to make the best of it and have a camp out in the backyard."

"Is that where Charlie is now? I have an incoming player I need to speak with him about."

"Nope. He's in the kitchen helping Jack with the dishes." Locky started to lead Chet towards the kitchen when laughter from outside the open French doors caught his attention. "I'd better go see who's having all the fun and put a stop to it," he said with a wink.

"It was nice to meet you." Chet wanted to apologise for ogling the man, but he didn't want to embarrass Locky anymore than he already had.

"You too," Locky replied on his way outside.

Chet knocked on the swinging kitchen door. Walking in on Charlie and his partner Jack in a compromising position wasn't on the agenda. "Hello?"

"Come in, Chet," Charlie called out.

Although blind, Charlie Salinger had quickly learned to recognise the sound of Chet's voice. It was just one of Charlie's skills that fascinated Chet. "Hope I'm not intruding," he said, entering the kitchen.

"Not at all." Charlie settled a stack of plates in a cabinet before turning towards Chet. "Jack and I were just talking about the food order he needs to place in the morning. We've got six new freshmen and your senior transfer coming in this week."

"Actually, that's what I wanted to talk to you about." Chet took a seat at the kitchen island. "I'm trying to find alternative housing for Bobby Ray Sikes."

Charlie's sightless eyes narrowed. "You have a problem with him living here?"

"To be honest, yes. Bobby Ray's not out of the closet to anyone but a handful of people. I think moving into BK is his way of declaring his sexuality, but I truly believe it'd be the worst move he could make. He's so close to getting drafted by a pro team."

"You think he should live a fucking lie just to play football? That they won't want him if they know he's gay?" Jack Hershie asked, throwing the dishcloth in the sink.

Chet held up his hands at the accusing expression on Jack's face. "Hey, I'm gay, remember? I'm not saying they won't want him, but he needs to learn discretion. If he plays his cards right, he'll be able to go pro and still enjoy his personal life, but not if his sexuality is shoved into the faces of fans and the media."

Jack turned back to the sink, but Chet could tell the former Marine still wasn't convinced. The last thing he'd wanted was to make his friends angry but frankly, protecting Bobby was his top priority.

"Anyway, I came by to see if either of you have a suggestion for alternative housing."

"Ask Demitri," Charlie said. "If anyone can find you a place, it'd be him."

"Thanks." Chet hated the thought of leaving with hard feelings between them. "It's nothing against BK House. I just want what's best for Bobby Ray."

"Sounds like the kid means something to you," Charlie replied.

"Yeah. I recruited him out of high school for UA. I gave his father my word I'd look after him, but then I quit and came here." Chet didn't go into further detail. "Anyway, I'd better get out of your hair and find Bobby Ray a place to live."

"Let us know if you need anything," Jack offered in a surprise move.

"I will. Thanks."

* * * *

Sitting across from Demitri Demakis, BK House founder and main contributor, Chet explained Bobby's situation. Finished, he lifted his beer to his lips and took a drink. "So, what do you think?"

Demitri glanced at his partner. "Did Dane ever find a roommate?"

Aaron Billings, NCIU's head soccer coach, shook his head. "Not sure, but I could give him a call."

"Dane Jefferson?" Chet asked. "I thought he graduated last year." Dane had been one of NCIU's top rated soccer players and as far as Chet knew, the guy wasn't gay.

"He did, but he's going to graduate school here. Let me give him a call."

Aaron walked into the house, leaving Demitri and Chet alone on the patio. "I don't know much about Dane. Is he a good kid?"

"One of the best," Demitri said. "He's quiet. Keeps to himself most of the time. He just bought a house, so I guess he's planning to stay in town after finishing his master's. I tried to get him to move into BK as an advisor, but he insisted that it was time he bought a place."

"I didn't know he was gay," Chet commented.

"Not many do. That's why he might just be the perfect roommate for Bobby Ray," Demitri said.

"If Dane's interested, how much do you think he'll want in rent? I don't know much about Bobby Ray's financial status, but he lost his dad last year, so things might be kinda tight at home."

Demitri grinned. "He bought the house from Tony Bianchi, paid cash. If he agrees to share space with Bobby Ray, I doubt rent will be a deciding factor."

The sliding glass door opened and Aaron stepped out onto the patio. "Dane said he'd consider it, but he wants to meet Bobby Ray before he makes a final decision."

"That's fair," Chet agreed. "He's due in town Thursday. If you can set up a meeting, I'll make sure he's there."

"How about a small barbecue on Thursday night? We could do it here at the house," Aaron offered. "Might be a nice way to introduce Bobby Ray to a few people."

"Sounds good." Hopefully Bobby would hit it off with Dane and Chet's problem would be solved.

* * * *

With his battered truck loaded with everything he'd need for the next year, Bobby pulled into town on Wednesday night and parked in the first empty lot he could find. His nerves and a constant supply of coffee were the only thing keeping him awake.

Bobby tapped his fingers on the steering wheel. Although he should probably just sleep in his truck again, the lure of seeing Chet Sloan and sleeping in a real bed was a temptation he couldn't deny. He pulled his prepaid phone out of the glove box and dialled Chet's number.

"Hello?" a sleepy voice answered.

"Chet?"

"Bobby Ray? Is there something wrong?"

"No. I just got to town and wondered if I could crash on your couch or something?"

"Wait. What? How'd you get here so fast?"

"I decided to drive straight through instead of spending money for a hotel." Bobby didn't mention the need to see Chet had spurred him into making the decision. "Anyway, is it okay if I come by?"

Chet went silent for several moments. "I'm not..." Chet sighed heavily into the phone. "I'm not sure that's a good idea."

Bobby had a feeling Chet would say no, so he was prepared. "Really? You'd rather I spent the night in my truck after driving for the last twenty-seven hours to get here?"

Once again, Chet sighed heavily. "No, of course not." After another moment of silence, he spoke again. "You have something to write on?"

"I'll punch it into the GPS Mom bought me." Bobby typed in the address as Chet rattled it off. "Got it."

"See you in about ten minutes."

"Thanks," Bobby replied. He powered down the phone and stuck it back into the glove box before starting the truck.

Although he couldn't wait to see Chet, he was under no illusion the man would immediately fall into his arms. It would take time for Chet to lower his walls enough for Bobby to sneak over them, but once he did, he wasn't about to let Chet get away from him a second time.

* * * *

Chet jumped out of bed and threw on a pair of sleep pants and a T-shirt. *What the fuck am I doing?* Whether it was the late hour or the fatigue he'd detected in Bobby's voice, he hadn't been strong enough to tell him no. He walked across the hall and opened the guest room door.

"Ah, shit." He'd forgotten about the state of the room. For weeks he'd been meaning to go through the boxes shipped from his sister Jenny after she'd sold their fathers' house. He briefly considered making Bobby sleep on the sofa, but in the end decided to hand over his own room for the night.

Chet closed the door securely and rushed to the living room. The room wasn't messy, but there were several empty beer cans along with a recent Playgirl magazine on the coffee table. He scooped them up and dashed into the kitchen.

After the cans were deposited in the recycling bin and the magazine stuffed in a drawer, Chet got to work loading the dishwasher. The doorbell rang before he got the last of the glasses taken care of and Chet made a mental note to clean his fucking house as soon as Bobby was settled with Dane.

On the way to the front door, Chet stopped and took a deep breath. He quickly ran through all the reasons he'd left Arizona in an effort to shore up his walls, but when the bell rang again, Chet was left more uncertain than he'd ever been.

He's just a kid, he reminded himself, reaching for the lock. *Oh fuck, not a kid at all*, he realised upon seeing Bobby for the first time in three years.

"Hey," Bobby said around a million dollar smile.

At a loss for words, Chet stepped back, allowing Bobby entrance into the house. The fresh-faced boy from Arkansas had been replaced by a man handsome enough to grace the pages of the magazine he'd jacked off to earlier. Bobby's heavy five o'clock shadow was testament to just how much he'd matured since they'd been apart.

"Chet? Are you okay?" Bobby asked, setting down a large duffle bag.

"Yeah. Of course." Chet tried to play off his inability to reconcile his sudden bout of lust with the first excuse he could come up with. "I was sleeping when you called. Guess I'm still pretty fuzzy."

"Sorry about that." Bobby hooked his thumbs into the front pockets of his jeans, drawing Chet's attention to his cock, and looked around the living room. "Nice house."

"Thanks." Turning away from the tempting outline trapped behind Bobby's zipper, Chet gestured towards the kitchen. "Can I get you something to drink?"

Bobby grinned. "I don't suppose you'd let me have a beer?"

"You suppose right," Chet grumbled. "Contributing to the delinquency..."

"I just turned twenty-two," Bobby said, cutting Chet off.

"Oh, right." Chet knew he could use conditioning as an excuse, but he wasn't naïve enough to believe his players didn't drink on occasion. "Just one."

Bobby followed Chet into the kitchen. "Mom said to tell you hi."

"How's she doing?" Chet asked, retrieving two cans of beer from the fridge. Bobby's mention of his mom helped to cool his thoughts of lust. Chet watched Bobby open his beer and take a big drink. The moment of distraction gave him a chance to look his fill. Where was the boy he'd gone fishing with? Admittedly, Chet had worried for years that his feelings for Bobby had more to do with his respect for the superstar who was more down to earth than any athlete he'd ever come into contact with. But watching Bobby drink the beer, Chet realised it was so much more. He was emotionally bonded to Bobby like he'd never been with another. What was it that Bobby possessed that no other man had ever come close to? Bobby swallowed and picked the conversation back up, bringing Chet out of his musings.

"Good, real good. I know it sounds bad, but I think she's happier than she's been in years. She joined some social group in Pine Bluff. I'm still not sure what all they do, but she leaves the house once a week wearing a stupid-looking red hat." Bobby shook his head and chuckled. "Dumbest damn hat I've ever seen, but I don't have the heart to tell her."

Chet tried to keep his eyes from roaming Bobby's body while he spoke, but failed miserably. Although Bobby looked older, his body appeared the same if not smaller than the last time Chet had seen him. *Held him.*

"Have you been keeping up with your conditioning regime?"

Bobby stared at the top of the can in his hand and slowly lifted it to his mouth without answering. Chet watched the muscles in Bobby's throat as he gulped the beer. It was obvious he was putting off an answer. "Bobby?"

Setting the empty can on the kitchen island, Bobby shook his head. "I've slacked off a bit this summer."

"Why would you do something like that? We both know it's gonna be hell getting those muscles built back up to where they need to be." Chet wondered if Bobby's father's death had affected him more than he'd let on.

"I know," Bobby mumbled. "But Coach Nelson told me NCIU has one of the best trainers around."

"True, but you've only got a week before practice starts." Something didn't feel right. "This isn't like you. Have you changed that much from the kid who used to eat, drink and breathe football?"

"I'll be ready! I've had a shitty year. Give me a fucking break, would ya?"

Bobby headed for the living room, but before he could get far, Chet reached out and grabbed the young man's forearm, pulling him up short. "You're right. I'm sorry about your dad. I lost mine two years ago and it still hurts every damn day. But you can't let that pain stand in the way of your future."

Bobby reached up and covered Chet's hand that still rested on his arm. "I could've really used your support last year," he whispered. "A lot happened, and I didn't have anyone to talk to."

"You were at Arizona for three years. Don't tell me you didn't make a single friend in all that time."

Bobby dropped his hand and pulled away from Chet's hold. "There were a few guys I kicked around with, but they weren't the kind of friends you'd open up to."

Chet hated the sadness in Bobby's dark brown eyes. "You could've called."

With a snort, Bobby walked over and picked up his duffle. "The phone goes both ways, Chet. You had to have known how much I needed you, but instead of reaching out you sent a hundred dollar bouquet of flowers to a funeral home." He gestured to the couch. "I'm dead on my feet. Is that my bed for the rest of the night?"

Chet shook his head. Not only had he let a player and friend down, but he'd hurt someone he loved because he was too chicken shit to face him. "Take my room. The guestroom's full of boxes, so I'll sleep there."

"You don't have to do that," Bobby protested.

Chet needed time to process his feelings. Shame warred with anger over Bobby's lack of conditioning. Add in the fact that he still had romantic feelings for Bobby, and Chet's emotions seemed to be all over the place. "Just take it."

* * * *

Bobby dropped his bag on the floor at the foot of Chet's bed and glanced around the room. If he didn't know better, he'd swear he was back in Chet's Arizona house. The curtains, bedspread and pictures were the same. Only the layout had changed.

A picture on Chet's dresser caught his attention. He walked over and lifted the eight by ten framed photo and smiled. It was Chet hoisting the shiny bowl trophy over his head, surrounded by his entire team.

Despite his sour mood, Bobby couldn't help but smile. He'd recorded the bowl game and had watched it close to a hundred times. It wasn't the game itself he'd been interested in, but the proud and confident coach who had stepped in to fill Coach Nelson's shoes at the last minute. It had been the highlight of Chet's career and Bobby hadn't been there to share it with him.

Setting the picture down, Bobby undressed and sat on the edge of the bed. He methodically unwrapped the elastic bandage from around his left knee and tossed it to the floor. He rubbed the sore and slightly swollen area and wondered again if he was making the right decision. Since injuring his anterior cruciate ligament, or ACL, ten weeks earlier, his recovery hadn't been what the doctors' had hoped. Without surgery to repair the partial tear of the ligament that helped stabilise his knee, Bobby would be in for weeks of rehabilitation. However, with surgery, he'd be out for the season for sure. It had been a hard choice, but opting for rehabilitation had seemed the most sensible choice.

After talking it over with his mom, Bobby had decided to continue with physical therapy. If he resorted to surgery, there'd be no way he could play football in his senior year, and getting the full-ride scholarship was imperative to finishing his education.

He lifted his bag onto his lap and searched for the bottle of massage oil. Coming up empty, it dawned on him he'd left it in the truck. "Shit."

Instead of redressing, Bobby scanned the room, looking for lotion or something. When he didn't see anything useful, he slid open the top drawer on the bedside table. Just as he'd suspected, he found lube. It took him several seconds to gather the nerve to remove the bottle from the drawer, but once he had his gaze landed on something even more interesting.

Bobby set the lube on the table and reached back into the drawer. He moved aside the flesh-coloured dildo and retrieved the picture. His hands started to shake as he stared at the photograph taken of him on the day of his high school graduation. It was obvious from the well-worn picture that it had been held often. The fact that it had been in the same drawer with the lube and dildo gave him hope.

He squashed the urge to run across the hall and question Chet about the picture, knowing Chet would only deny he still had sexual thoughts about him. "I know your secret," he whispered to the photograph on the dresser. Coach or not, Chet was still a man, and Bobby had seduced several of them in the previous three years.

After carefully replacing the photograph, Bobby picked up the lube and went to work massaging his knee. He needed to come up with a plan of action, and what better place to do it than Chet's bed.

Chapter Three

Chet glanced at the closed bedroom door. It was nearing three o'clock in the afternoon and Bobby had yet to emerge. He hated to wake him. It was obvious the man needed his sleep, but they were going to be late. Lifting his hand, Chet rapped his knuckles against the door. "Bobby?"

When he received no answer, he opened the door. Before he could call the name again, his gaze landed on a nude body tangled in the sheets, his sheets. Chet bit his bottom lip. Knowing it was wrong, he tried to step back and shut the door, but his feet wouldn't budge.

Chet's eyebrows drew together when he figured out what was so different. Bobby hadn't merely slacked off on his training, he was downright thin. His worry overrode everything else. He tossed the blanket over Bobby's bare hip, hiding the tempting ass from view before sitting on the bed. "Time to get up," he said, eyeing the bottle of lube on the table. *Had Bobby gone through his drawers?* "Bobby!" he said with heat.

With a groan, Bobby rolled over and opened his big brown eyes. Spotting Chet beside him, he smiled. "Morning."

"Afternoon," Chet corrected. He reached out and grabbed the lube. "Did you go through my things?" Knowing exactly what had been in the drawer with the lube, Chet wavered between embarrassment and fury.

"Sorry," Bobby mumbled. "My legs were cramping after driving so far. I have massage oil, but I left it in my truck. I'll buy you another bottle."

"That's not the point and you know it." Chet gestured towards the door. "Don't read anything into what you found in there."

Bobby rubbed the sleep from his eyes and sat up. "I meant no harm, I swear it. I was just too tired to go back out to the truck."

With his lips puffy from sleep, Bobby was a temptation hard to resist. Chet's anger over the invasion of privacy melted away. "I need you to jump in the shower. We've been invited to a barbecue at Demitri Demakis' house. I thought it'd be a good opportunity for you to meet your potential roommate."

"I'm up for meeting people, but I've been giving it a lot of thought, and I'd still like to move into BK House." Chet opened his mouth to protest, but Bobby held his hand up in an effort to silence him. "I won't go blabbing it around campus. The press didn't give a shit where I lived for three years. Why do you think they'd care now?"

"Because of what BK is and who you are," Chet answered. He reached out and wrapped his hand around Bobby's ankle. "I promise you, I have your best interests at heart."

"I know."

"The guy I want you to meet today is a graduate student by the name of Dane Jefferson. He's gay and he owns his own house. According to Demitri, Dane probably wouldn't expect much in rent money." Even as he said the words, Chet could tell they weren't doing anything to change Bobby's mind. "Why're you so adamant about living in BK?"

Bobby readjusted the blankets around his waist. "I read this article in a magazine. It said BK House was a great place for young gay men to get the support they need." Bobby pressed his palm to his bare chest. "I want that. I wanna know what it feels like to be in an environment where I can talk to people and not be afraid I might out myself. I know you want me locked away where the press won't find out I like a man's dick up my ass, but there's more to me than football. Why can't you understand that?"

Chet swallowed around the lump in his throat. If he were honest with himself, he knew Bobby was right. He was more than just a football player, but it was this that kept him at arm's length. Images of Bobby on a bed with another man's cock buried in his ass didn't sit well either. Chet had been stupid to think Bobby would reach the age of twenty-two a virgin. Still...

Chet rose and walked towards the door. "I don't want to hear about all the boys you've let fuck you," he grumbled over his shoulder.

"Not boys, men."

Chet stopped and turned around.

"Men I thought were like you, but it turned out they were nothing like you. They didn't care about me or have my best interests at heart. All they wanted was to fuck Bobby Ray Sikes. They didn't give a shit about Bobby." Bobby bit his bottom lip and scooted to the edge of the bed. "They weren't you and they should've been."

Chet started to reach for Bobby but shoved his hands in his pockets instead. "Hop in the shower. We need to be out of here in thirty minutes."

* * * *

With his knee still bothering him after the long drive, Bobby had opted to rewrap it and wear jeans. As he rode in the passenger seat of Chet's SUV, he began to regret his decision. "I thought it was supposed to be cooler up here."

"Normally it is, but Mother Nature doesn't always follow the rules." Chet pulled in front of a large house. A small sign by the front step read BK House. "What're we doing here? I thought we were late to the party thing?"

"I called Aaron, Demitri's partner, and told him we'd be a little late. I thought you should get a look at BK before you blow Dane off this afternoon."

"I wouldn't blow him off anyway. I may be stubborn, but I'm not an asshole," he mumbled, opening his door.

Chet joined Bobby on the sidewalk leading to the house. "I know you wouldn't. I just meant you should make an informed decision."

Although Chet hadn't mentioned their earlier conversation, Bobby could tell it was still on his mind. It was a good thing, in his opinion. He may not have meant to bring up his past lovers, but he hadn't missed the expression of jealousy on Chet's face when he had. Good. How many nights had he sat up wondering if Chet was sleeping beside some guy?

"Charlie and Jack are already at Demitri's, but Locky, the new guy, agreed to come back to give you a tour." Chet reached out and rang the doorbell.

"Cool."

Chet glanced down. "Are you limping?"

Fuck. Bobby shrugged. "You drive from Arkansas to Idaho and see if you aren't sore."

"No thanks. Any more than a couple hours and I go into some kinda trance." He grinned. "I still can't believe you didn't get a hotel room along the way." Chet's hand went to the small of Bobby Ray's back and he almost melted right there on the stoop.

Before Bobby Ray could fully enjoy the moment, the front door opened. *Damn.* "Hello," he said automatically.

The handsome man smiled and held out his hand. "You must be Bobby Ray. Locky Regent."

"Nice to meet you," Bobby replied, shaking Locky's hand.

Locky nodded in Chet's direction. "Good to see you again."

"You, too," Chet said.

Locky ushered them into the house and closed the door. "We finally got the a/c fixed, but I think it's going to take a while for the house to cool down to where it should be." Locky gestured towards the large open room. "Obviously, this is the living room," he said, beginning the tour.

Bobby followed Locky around the house while Chet watched the end of the baseball game he'd started at home. "How many guys live here?"

"We have twenty-two, including you. There were a lot of freshmen requesting placement at BK this year, but we just don't have the room."

"You mean there's a waiting list or something?" Bobby had waited until the last possible moment to make the call to Coach Nelson about transferring. He hated the thought that he'd jumped to the front of the list because of who he was.

Locky chuckled. "Yep, but Demitri's come up with a solution." He led Bobby into a huge room. "This is our newest addition. It's a place for residents and non-residents to gather and hang out."

Bobby liked that idea. "So you don't have to live here to come by?"

"Right. Demitri's been talking to one of BK's biggest supporters, Tony Bianchi, about building another house on the other side of campus, but until then, he wanted a refuge for students to get away to if they needed."

Bobby nodded. "I imagine that magazine article brought a lot of attention to BK. I know this place is one of the reasons I wanted to transfer." He looked around the room. There were several groupings of over-stuffed furniture, a huge television mounted on the wall and a small kitchenette in the far corner. "Looks nice."

"We think so." Locky gestured to a door. "That's the study room. There are desks and computers in there in case you need the quiet. All courtesy of Tony Bianchi."

BK House was everything Bobby had hoped for and more. Unfortunately, the guilt started to set in as they wound up the tour. Before they arrived back in the living room, Bobby stopped walking and cleared his throat. "If I do what Coach Sloan wants and move in with this Dane guy, would I still be able to come here if I wanted?"

"Absolutely."

"And you'll be able to move one of those incoming freshmen up on the list?"

"Yep." Locky put a hand on Bobby's shoulder. "Charlie explained your situation to me, and I think we can work around it. I can't promise the press won't find out you're coming here on occasion, but I'll do my best to make sure the residents understand the importance of discretion."

"Thanks." Although he still needed to meet Dane, Bobby felt much better about his options. Knowing he could enjoy the camaraderie BK had to offer was the most important thing. It also might help get him back in Chet's good graces. "Can I let you know this evening?"

Locky smiled. "Sure. That sounds fair."

* * * *

Chet pulled away from BK and back onto the street. "So what'd you think?"

"I like it. Locky's nice." Bobby glanced at Chet. "He made me feel welcome."

Just how welcome, Chet wondered to himself. As soon as Bobby disappeared down the hall with Locky, Chet fought the urge to run after them. Maybe it was their earlier conversation, but since learning Bobby had a thing for older men instead of guys his own age, Chet doubted he'd ever feel comfortable having Bobby around his single friends. "So you like Locky?"

"Yeah, like I told you, he's nice." Bobby reached over and punched Chet playfully on the arm. "Jealous?"

"Maybe. Although I know I have no right to be," Chet admitted.

"Well don't be. I didn't transfer my senior year to pick up on Locky." Bobby was silent for a moment before slapping the seat beside him. "Shit. Are you already involved with someone?"

"No." The elephant in the front seat was suddenly too big to handle. Chet had done everything he could to get Bobby out of his system, but if it hadn't happened in three years with several states between them, he doubted it was possible.

He found a shady spot to park two houses down from Demitri's and pulled up to the kerb. Shutting the engine off, Chet unbuckled his seat belt and turned to face Bobby. "I can't coach you at practice and fuck you at night. It's not right. It's not who I am. I'm not saying I don't want you because I think we both know that'd be a damn lie, but my job means a lot to me." Chet reached out and cupped Bobby's face. "But the future you've worked so hard for means more and I can't take the risk."

Bobby's eyes drifted shut as he turned his head to place a kiss on Chet's palm. "What if I didn't play ball? Would you still feel the same way?"

"If you're asking whether my feelings would be the same if you weren't the Bobby Ray Sikes every pro scout's been following for years, the answer would be yes. But you're not that person, Bobby. You have a gift, and I can't let my feelings get in the way of what you were born to do." Although Chet was confident in his own feelings, Bobby was still young. He had a lot of living to do before he'd be ready to make a life-altering decision like the one he seemed to be contemplating. He dropped his hand and pulled the key from the ignition.

"I'm glad you and every other football fan in the nation have my future all mapped out for me.

Otherwise I might be stuck doing what I want to do instead of what I'm supposed to do."

It was remarks like that that reminded Chet of Bobby's youth. He was grateful when he saw another car pull up behind him. "Locky's here. We'd better drop this for now and join the party."

"Yeah, whatever," Bobby mumbled as he opened the door.

* * * *

After a short introduction, Bobby took a seat next to Dane in the shade. He gestured to the open book on Dane's lap. "What're you reading?"

Dane held up his book. "Ancient Native Tribes of the Southeast United States. My professor, Magnus Sofokleous, wrote it."

Bobby couldn't imagine bringing a boring book to a barbecue. He wondered just how much Dane really wanted to be there. "Not to sound stupid or anything, but is that archaeology?"

Dane pushed his small horn-rimmed glasses up and shook his head. "Actually, it's anthropology, the study of humans and how they developed over time. Archaeology is the study of material artefacts."

"Oh, okay." Bobby nodded. "I'm working towards a degree in social work. Some people say it's an easy degree, but I like the courses. I figure if I can help people and enjoy doing it, I'm ahead of the game."

Dane locked at Bobby over his glasses for a moment. "Yeah, I can see you doing that." He marked his place then shut his book and set it carefully in the leather messenger bag beside his chair. "As you can tell, I'm not real comfortable with people. When I was eight my mom signed me up for soccer. I guess she thought

I'd come out of my shell if I was part of a team, but it didn't really work. I like to play, and I guess I'm pretty good at it, but I do it more for physical exercise than anything else. 'Course now I have a pool, so I just stick to swimming most days." Dane blushed. "Sorry. I guess you didn't ask me about soccer, did you?"

Although Dane was obviously intelligent, Bobby got the idea he was more than a little socially awkward. "That's okay. It's all part of getting to know someone."

"Yeah." Dane looked around before leaning in to whisper, "Not many people take the time to get to know me. It seems I'm not smart enough to hang with the intellectuals and not tough enough to hang with the jocks." He shrugged. "But that's okay. I learned at an early age to entertain myself." He reached down and tapped the messenger bag. "That's why I bring books everywhere I go."

Bobby rubbed his jaw. Dane was a puzzle he might enjoy figuring out. "So are you looking for a roommate?"

"Looking? No. But I wouldn't mind sharing the house with someone. It's way too big for one person anyway." Dane pushed up his glasses again. "Oh, unless you're afraid of dogs. My parents bought me a German shepherd for a graduation present. Ares is supposed to be a guard dog, but he's a big softy."

"I like dogs." Bobby also found he quite liked Dane, despite his quirks. He almost hated to bring up how much living at Dane's house was going to cost him, but it would be the deciding factor.

"Then we're good," Dane said.

"Well, we still need to talk about the money. I get a small housing allowance from my scholarship and my mom tries to send me what she can each month, but I have to be honest, it isn't much."

Dane waved his hand. "The money's not important, so whatever your scholarship pays is fine with me."

Satisfied he could afford the change in housing, Bobby stuck out his hand. "Then if you'll have me, I'd love to be your new roomy."

"Don't you want to look at the house first?"

"Nope. As long as I'll be warm in the winter and cool in the summer, I'm good."

* * * *

From his position on the deck, Chet watched Bobby and Dane. "I need you to do me a favour."

"Sure," Julian answered, taking a drink of his iced tea.

"I think something's going on with Bobby Ray's conditioning routine. I noticed this morning that he seems thinner than he was three years ago." Chet turned his attention away from Bobby to look at Julian. "He said he'd been slacking lately, but I think it's more than that."

Julian rubbed the back of his neck. By the expression on his face it was obvious he was uncomfortable about something. "Not sure if you noticed, but he's favouring his left leg."

Chet nodded. "I noticed. He said it was just sore from riding in the truck for so many hours."

"Doesn't make sense. When you're driving it's the right leg that takes the workout."

"See if he'll talk to you about it. He practically snapped my head off earlier when I asked."

"I figured with him transferring you'd get that stick out of your ass and tell him how you feel."

Julian was the closest friend Chet had at NCIU and the only one he'd told about his strange relationship with Bobby. He couldn't imagine the rest of the faculty finding out he'd fallen in love with a boy straight out of high school. "He may be older now, but he's still got a future to look forward to. One that I can't really be a part of, so what's the point?"

Julian turned in his chair and leaned towards Chet. "The point is you love him. And if that hasn't gone away in the last three years, I doubt it's going away now that he's here. Stop living life afraid of the future and enjoy the now, dude."

Chet sat back in his chair in an effort to get his friend the hell out of his face. "What if acting on my feelings ruins his future? Do you really think I could live with myself if that happened?"

"So you're condemning Bobby Ray to a future of not being loved? Do you honestly think he'll get drafted and give up men? That's bullshit and you know it. He'll find himself in love somewhere along the way, whether it's with you or not is your choice."

The thought of Bobby loving and being loved by another man had Chet rethinking the argument he'd held onto for the past three years. "And the college? How would they handle a head coach fucking a player?"

Julian laughed. "I may not be a head coach, but I've been fucking Koby since he was a freshman and no one's had an issue because I've never made it one."

Chet scanned the area. There were several partnerships within his circle of friends that included teacher and student or coach and student. Julian was right. The college administration didn't get involved in its employees' personal lives unless they became a problem.

Julian turned serious. "I know your mom was a lot younger than your dad, but you can't let the fact that it didn't work cloud your judgement."

"I'll think about it," Chet said in an effort to get Julian to back down. He hated to be reminded of the way his mom had given birth to two children before deciding she was too young to settle down and have a family. "In the meantime, will you find out what's going on with Bobby's conditioning routine?"

"Yep. I've got an idea, but first I need to find Koby." Julian stood and started to walk off but stopped and turned back to Chet. "One word of advice. You'll have to learn to separate your love life from your job as his coach. In love you're both equal. Don't treat him at home like you'd treat him on the field."

For Chet, the statement drew an image of him fucking Bobby on the fifty yard line. "I should hope not."

* * * *

Dane shouldered his messenger bag and handed Bobby a slip of paper. "Here's the address. Just come by with your stuff later this evening or in the morning, either way is fine with me."

"You're leaving?" Bobby asked.

"Yeah. I really just came to meet you. I don't really know anyone else here except Coach Aaron and Demitri."

Bobby stood and held out his hand. "Thanks for everything you're doing for me."

Dane shook Bobby's hand and smiled. "Actually, I'm looking forward to having someone else in the house to talk to besides Ares."

Bobby released Dane's hand and watched him walk away.

"Is that going to work out?" Koby asked, striding up with Julian at his side.

"I hope so. Locky, at BK House, said I could still hang out there if I wanted to, so I figured it'd be easier this way. No sense in pissing off the coach before practice starts."

"You're right about that, although Coach Sloan's a great guy to play for." Koby plopped down in the grass in front of Bobby's chair. "I came over to ask if you wanted to go running with Julian and me in the morning? We usually get out around six before the traffic starts and go three or four miles depending on what we did the night before."

Any other time, Bobby would be jumping at the chance to run with the two men, but he knew his knee wasn't up to the exertion. "Thanks, but I've still got to get settled in at Dane's."

"Okay, maybe the next day then. Like I said, we run every morning." Julian cleared his throat and Koby grinned. "Well, except for Sundays. That's kind of our day to sleep in."

"Actually, I haven't been doing a lot of running lately. I've been focusing more on exercises." *Shit.* Bobby bit his bottom lip. He could tell by Julian's expression he didn't buy the excuse. Bobby knew he was going to have to come clean with the team trainer sooner or later, but he'd hoped to at least start practices first.

"Why don't you come into the weight room Monday morning and we'll work up a conditioning schedule?" Julian asked, speaking for the first time since he'd sat down.

With practice starting on Wednesday, Bobby knew he couldn't refuse. "Sure."

Julian stood and pulled Koby to his feet. "Good. I'll block off ten to noon for you."

"Great," Bobby replied, trying to plaster an enthusiastic smile on his face. As soon as Julian and Koby left, Bobby closed his eyes and rested his head on the back of the chair. He was so screwed.

* * * *

"I'm not used to seeing you like that," Bobby said from the passenger seat on the way home.

"Like what?" Chet asked. After his conversation with Julian, Chet began to feel more comfortable with his feelings for Bobby. He still hadn't worked out how to successfully straddle the line between coach and lover, but he was on the way.

"Laughing. Happy." Bobby scratched a fresh mosquito bite on his arm. "Is it just being around me that makes you grouchy?"

"You don't make me grouchy. You make me want things I thought I couldn't have," he tried to explain. He pulled around Bobby's beat-up truck at the end of the driveway and pushed the automatic garage door opener.

"What you *thought* you couldn't have? As in past tense?" Bobby released his seatbelt as Chet pulled into the garage.

A discussion between them was three years overdue and the last thing Chet wanted was to hold it in the damn garage. "Let's go inside." He'd never been much of a talker when it came to his feelings. The bits of information Julian knew were probably the most he'd ever opened up to anyone. As he climbed out of the SUV and unlocked the door to the house, Chet tried to organise his thoughts. He didn't have a clue how to even start.

The moment they were inside, Chet did what he'd been dying to do for years. He pressed Bobby against the door and kissed him. He'd held himself back for too long to be coy. Chet pushed his tongue past Bobby's lips to the warmth inside.

Bobby moaned into the kiss and thrust against him.

Oh, shit. Chet felt the hard ridge of Bobby's erection as it continued to bump and slide against him. The kiss had already turned sloppy with both of their tongues battling for dominance. It was like a dam had broken and all of Chet's hidden desires came pouring out. He felt Bobby's hands on his zipper and reached down to stop him. "We need to talk."

Bobby shook his head. "Not now."

Chet attempted to capture Bobby's hands as he continued to try and unzip Chet's shorts. "Not here. Not our first time."

"Get naked. Then I'll know you're serious," Bobby said, pulling off his shirt.

Chet pulled off his shirt and tossed it to the floor then pushed his shorts down to join it. He took a step back and crossed his arms over his chest. "Now you."

Bobby unzipped his jeans and started to take them off but stopped when they were at mid-thigh.

"What's wrong?" Chet teased. "I thought you were ready to get naked?"

"I am, but I just realised I need to pee."

Chet laughed and reached down to pull Bobby's jeans back up to his hips. "Then I guess you'd better take care of that." He turned Bobby and nudged him towards the door. "I'll be in the bedroom."

He followed Bobby down the hall, trying his best to keep his hands to himself. "Don't take too long or I might chicken out."

"Two minutes," Bobby said, disappearing into the bathroom.

Chet entered his bedroom and shook his head at the state of the unmade bed. He pushed the bedspread to the floor, remaking the bed with just the sheet. By the time Bobby joined him, Chet was starting to have doubts. Bobby was naked except for the bundled jeans in his hands hiding his groin. "Maybe we're taking things too fast. We should probably talk about a few things first."

Bobby dropped his jeans to the floor, exposing himself to Chet's view. "No talking until after you fuck me. I've waited too long to screw things up with words." He climbed onto the bed and rested his clasped hands behind his head.

The little shit's body was too tempting to ignore, especially after the years spent fantasising about Bobby being naked and in his bed. Chet pulled open the bedside drawer and removed the lube Bobby had used the previous night. "Are you sure massage oil was all you used this for?"

Bobby nodded. "Can you imagine how pissed you would've been if you'd come in here this morning and found my cum all over your sheets?"

Chet lifted one knee to the mattress and trailed his hand down the centre of Bobby's chest, stopping an inch away from the head of his cock where it rested on his stomach. "I don't think mad would be the word I'd use."

"Really? Tell me?" Bobby asked, moving higher so his cock brushed against Chet's fingers.

"Turned on," Chet whispered, moving Bobby's hand to his own cock. "Show me what you would've done. Let me see how you like to be touched."

Bobby's hand wrapped around his cock just below the head and squeezed. "You like to watch men jack off?"

Chet sat on the bed and poured several drops of lube onto his fingers. "No," he answered, moving his hand to Bobby's ass. "But I'd like to watch you do it. I've wondered if you touch yourself while thinking about me."

Bobby moaned when Chet stuck the tip of his finger into his hole. "All the time," Bobby confessed, moving his hand up and down on his cock. "I had a private dorm room the last two years just so I could come home from practice and jerk off."

Chet inserted another finger, watching for any sign of discomfort. "And what did you think about when you beat your meat?"

"You fucking me. Usually I had one hand around my dick and my fingers in my ass, just like you're doing," Bobby panted as Chet introduced a third finger.

While he had Bobby in a state of excitement, he needed a few answers. "How many men did you let fuck you?"

"Too many and not enough to make me forget you. What about you? How many men have you been with in the last three years?"

"Just one," he admitted, withdrawing his fingers. He opened the drawer and removed a strip of condoms, tossing them onto the bed after ripping one off.

"Do you still see him?" Bobby asked, uncertainty replacing desire.

"All the time, but not in my bed." Chet rolled the condom down his aching length and climbed onto the bed between Bobby's spread thighs.

"Who is he?"

Chet shook his head and directed his cock to Bobby's hole. "No more talking." He didn't want his first time with Bobby ruined by memories of his short affair with Magnus.

Bobby lifted his legs to drape over Chet's shoulders, worry still etched on his handsome face.

Chet pushed inside, wanting nothing more than to replace that expression with the need he'd witnessed earlier. He should probably tell Bobby about Magnus to ease his mind, but knowing the name behind the one man he'd let dominate him wouldn't be wise.

"Harder," Bobby urged, jacking his cock faster.

After withdrawing his cock, Chet thrust back inside deep and hard enough to move Bobby up the mattress several inches. It was in stark contrast to the way he felt. For three years he'd wanted to wrap his arms around Bobby and protect him from the bigots Chet knew would love to destroy him. *And here I am fucking him to the point of pain,* he acknowledged when he saw Bobby flinch.

Chet slowed his thrusts and lowered himself to lie on top of Bobby. "Let me make love to you."

Bobby winced and removed his legs from Chet's shoulders. "I thought that's what you were doing?"

Chet grinned. "Sure, but it's not the way I've always dreamed of making love to you." He swivelled his hips on the down stroke, grinding his groin against Bobby. "Do you still like to collect autographs from your favourite players?"

Bobby nodded.

"Good, because I have a couple for you in my closet. I met a few Chargers when I was in San Diego for the bowl game."

"For real?"

"Yep. See, even if I wasn't with you it didn't mean you weren't on my mind." Chet reached between them and covered Bobby's hand. He stared into Bobby's eyes as he helped stroke his cock. He was close, but coming before Bobby wasn't an option. He rose up and stared down at the beautiful body under him. "Show me."

With his nostrils flared, Bobby buried his head back into the fluffy down pillow and opened his mouth in a silent cry as the first strand of cum shot from his cock. "Chet," he gasped as three more strands splashed white pearls onto his stomach.

"Beautiful," Chet whispered as he released his own seed. Never would he forget the sight of Bobby at that moment. Suddenly, he wanted to bare his soul, and wash away his sins in the loving gaze of a twenty-two-year-old man. "I was too ashamed to come to your dad's funeral," he confessed.

"I needed you." Bobby winced once again when he straightened his legs.

"That's the third time you've done that."

"What?" Bobby asked, running his fingers through Chet's hair.

"Am I hurting you?" Chet pulled out and sat back on his heels. He removed the condom and tied it off before dropping it into the trashcan beside the bed.

"No," Bobby said, leaning up on his elbows. "I'm just not used to being folded in half like a taco shell."

For some reason the analogy struck Chet as funny. He dropped to Bobby's side and pulled the younger man against him. "Your folks trusted me to do what was best for you, and I betrayed them."

"Yes, you did," Bobby agreed, drawing his fingers through Chet's chest hair.

Although Chet knew he had, it was hard to hear. "I know."

"No, I don't think you do. I remember the conversation you had with my mom at my graduation party. She made you promise to take care of me if she sent me off to Arizona and you told her you would." Bobby pinched Chet's nipple hard enough to bring tears to Chet's eyes. "But then you left me in a city where I didn't know another soul."

"I kissed you," Chet tried to explain. "You were only eighteen. Your parents trusted me as a guardian, not a lover."

"Did they say that?" Bobby shook his head. "Because I don't remember that part. I think you're making up stuff now just to get out of feeling guilty."

Chet rubbed Bobby's back. "Have you always been this argumentative or is this something you picked up in the last three years?"

Bobby leaned up to stare down at Chet. "You can say what you want, but you really only know Bobby Ray Sikes from Star City Arkansas. You may call me Bobby now, but you still think of me as that hick you took to the city for the first time. I'm not that guy anymore."

"What're you saying?" Chet asked.

"That maybe you should take the time to get to know Bobby, college senior and soon to be social worker."

Chapter Four

Bobby stood in front of the large house and swallowed around the lump in his throat. "Holy shit." He glanced at the ripped and stained recliner in the back of his truck and cringed. "I'm gonna need to know where the town dump is."

"Don't be ridiculous." Chet led the way to the massive front doors. "I knew Dane bought a house from Tony, but I didn't realise it was actually Tony's house."

The door opened and eighty pounds of growling fur stepped out ahead of Dane. "Ares. Sit," Dane commanded. The German shepherd immediately obeyed and sat back on his haunches. "Sorry about that."

"Don't be," Bobby replied. "Ares is just doing his job." He bent and held his hand out for the guard dog to sniff. Satisfied that he wouldn't be eaten during the night, Bobby stood and addressed Dane. "I hope I came at a good time."

"Perfect. The cleaning crew just left." Dane stepped back and called Ares to his side. "Come in."

Bobby stepped into the large marble foyer and gawked like a kid entering Disneyland for the first time. How would he be able to fit into the world Dane obviously came from?

"Quite a place," Chet remarked, resting a hand on the small of Bobby's back.

Dane blushed. "Please don't think badly of me. I was brought up to make sound investment decisions in everything I buy, and my accountant told me this place was under-priced."

"I don't think badly of you at all," Bobby said. "I'll just have to remember to keep my socks picked up."

Dane laughed and led them up a wide staircase that seemed to curve around for no other reason than looks. "Why do you think I had an entire crew here cleaning this morning?"

Bobby reached the second floor and waited for Chet before following Dane down the hallway.

Dane opened the first door before moving to the next. "You can take your pick of rooms. This one has a better view, but the one at the end of the hall is a lot bigger."

Bobby glanced into the first room. A large set of French doors led out to a small balcony overlooking a private lake. "You weren't kidding about the view. I'll take this one."

"Don't you want to at least see the other one?" Dane asked from the doorway.

Turning away from the view, Bobby shook his head. "This one's three times bigger than what I'm used to. I can't imagine what I'd do with more than this."

Chet whispered in Bobby's ear. "I'll get you the address of the dump."

"No kidding," Bobby whispered back. The room was equipped with a large four-poster bed and a small sitting area done entirely in white. The couch and accompanying chairs looked like big clouds floating in the centre of the room.

"Would you rather have a tour of the rest of the house first or bring in your things?" Dane asked, still standing in the doorway.

"Why don't we go ahead and unload. Coach Sloan has a meeting he needs to get to in an hour," Bobby told his new roommate.

Dane nodded and disappeared out of the doorway. Bobby turned to Chet. "Can you believe this place?"

"It's something all right. One day you'll be able to afford a house like this, though."

Bobby knew that wasn't the case, but he was fine living on a social worker's salary. "I don't need anything this big to be happy."

* * * *

After several minutes of making out with Chet in his new bedroom, Bobby watched Chet's SUV disappear down the driveway. He sighed and closed the front door. Because Chet's meeting would probably run late and it was Bobby's first night in his new home, they'd agreed to meet for lunch the following day.

"Dane?" he called, walking towards the back of the house. He hadn't had his tour yet, but Dane had excused himself to his study after they'd carried the last box in. "Dane?"

"In here," Dane answered.

Bobby rounded a corner and came to a short hallway. The doors were open so he glanced inside the rooms until he found Dane, Ares sitting close by.

Unlike everything else in the house, Dane's study seemed in complete disarray. Books and papers were strewn on every available surface, making it difficult to concentrate on the lone man standing in front of a wall of books. "Chet just left," he announced.

Dane glanced over his shoulder. "He seems nice." He pulled a ratty-looking leather bound book from the shelf and turned around. "Am I wrong in thinking the two of you are more than coach and player?"

Although it was the first time since he'd arrived that someone had asked, Bobby knew it wouldn't be the last. "No, you're not wrong. I've known him since I was in high school."

Dane's blond eyebrows rose. "You've dated since you were a teenager?"

Bobby shook his head and headed out of the claustrophobic room. "I'll tell you all about it over a bottle of water."

Dane followed Bobby into the kitchen and set his book on the breakfast table before retrieving two bottles of water from the fridge. Within seconds, Ares was once again at Dane's side. Ares might not be the world's best guard dog from what Bobby had seen, but he was truly devoted to his master.

"I hope you don't think I'm being too nosy. You know you don't have to tell me anything if you don't want to," Dane said.

"No, that's okay. If we're going to live together, you should know why Chet wants to keep the fact that we'll be dating quiet." Bobby went on to explain the strained relationship and their hours-old reconciliation. "Although I know he loves me, I want him to get to know the person I've become and not who I was."

"And how's he supposed to do that if you have to hide the fact you're dating?" Dane asked, pushing his glasses up.

"He wants to hide it, not me," Bobby clarified. He rubbed his hands together, making a decision to share his secret with Dane. It would be too hard to hide his injury from Dane if they were living together. "Chet doesn't know it yet, but my future in football is seriously doubtful."

"Huh?"

Bobby took a deep breath. "I have a partially torn ACL. It happened two days before finals last semester."

Dane's jaw dropped. "You had surgery less than three months ago and you're planning to play this season?"

Bobby shook his head. Soccer players were just as susceptible to ACL tears as football players, so he was sure Dane was familiar with the injury. "No. At first the doctor thought the tear might heal on its own if I rested it, but by the time he suggested surgery, it was too late to have it and still be ready for the season."

"So you're planning to play anyway?" Dane shook his head. "That could really mess you up."

"I know," Bobby acknowledged. "But if I don't play, I don't get my scholarship. If I can make it through at least part of the season I don't think they'll take the scholarship away."

"But if you have the surgery there's an excellent chance of full recovery before the draft."

Bobby had been over every possible scenario and they all led to the same conclusion. "Do you really think a running back coming off ACL surgery will be picked up in the draft after having sat out his senior year? Especially a player who refuses to live life in the closet? I doubt it, and that's why finishing my degree is so important to me."

"What does Coach Sloan say about it?"

"He doesn't know. It would put him in a bad position if I did. He'd be torn between telling the scholarship committee and letting me play injured."

"Yeah, but you'd also be deceiving him. How do you think he'll take it once he finds out you've been lying?"

Bobby crossed his arms on the table and buried his face in the pocket they created. "I don't know."

"Excuse me if I'm crossing the line, but how do you expect him to get to know the man you've become if you're lying to him?"

Good question.

* * * *

Bobby decided to wait until after his conditioning appointment with Julian before making a final decision on whether or not to tell Chet about his knee.

He entered the weight room and glanced around, impressed. "You've got a lot of state-of-the-art equipment in here."

Julian slowed the treadmill to a stop and stepped off. "Yeah. After we won the Holiday Bowl, corporate donations came pouring in, including three VertiMax systems." Julian grinned. "Guess what I'm going to have you working on?"

"The VertiMax?" Bobby guessed. He'd worked out on one of the elastic band resistance strengthening machines before but not since his injury.

"Yep." Julian stared Bobby in the eyes. "You think you can handle that?"

Since his injury, Bobby had tried to keep a good regimen of prescribed exercises like hamstring curls and shallow standing knee bends, but he knew his knee wasn't up to jumping up and down on the VertiMax.

It soon became obvious by the challenging expression on Julian's face he knew something was wrong with Bobby's knee. He stared back at Julian for several moments before answering. "No, and something gives me the feeling you already know that."

"Okay then, follow me." Julian turned and walked towards an office in the corner of the exercise area.

Julian motioned for Bobby to shut the door. "Drop the sweats and have a seat," he said, indicating the treatment table. The muscles in Julian's jaw ticked, broadcasting his anger, so Bobby didn't question him.

In nothing but his T-shirt and a pair of underwear, Bobby sat on the training table and stretched his injured leg out. At that point he figured there was little reason to hide his injury. The big question was what Julian would do about it.

Julian greased his hands with massage oil before walking to the table. "Knee?"

Bobby nodded. "ACL partial tear almost eleven weeks ago."

Julian massaged Bobby's knee while he spoke. "So you knew about it when you called Justin?"

Bobby nodded again. "I can play. Up until a week ago, I was getting physical therapy. I may not be able to run at my normal speed, but I won't slack off on training or therapy. As soon as the season's over, I'll have surgery if the doctor still advises it."

"You know we can't let you play without a doctor's release, right?"

Bobby had rarely begged for anything, but he was prepared to do whatever it took to earn Julian's faith. "I'll work my ass off, I promise. Just give me two more weeks to heal, and I'll go to whatever doctor you want."

Julian narrowed his eyes and wiped his hands on a towel. "Do you want to go pro so badly you'd risk damaging your knee even more than it is in order to play this year?"

"No. I want a degree. I can't get it without the scholarship," he admitted.

With his hands on his hips, Julian dropped his head and muttered to himself for several moments. "Can you run at all?"

"Yeah. I haven't gone full barrel yet, but I've jogged on the treadmill and I've tried to get in at least twenty minutes on the elliptical every day." Bobby shrugged. "Well, before I left home anyway."

"If you've been doing that, why're your muscles showing signs of atrophy?"

"Because I'm afraid of overdoing it, so I haven't pushed myself. Before I got hurt, I ran five miles a day and worked on strength training at least two hours a day. There's no way I could keep up that schedule with my knee the way it is."

Julian bent over and picked up Bobby's shorts. "Put these back on and meet me at the treadmill."

* * * *

By the time he finished with Julian's workout, Bobby was in some serious pain, but he pasted a smile on his face and headed for the shower. He dropped his clothes on the locker room bench and grabbed a towel from the rack.

Bobby groaned as the warm water hit him. He tilted his face up to the spray and let the tears fall. Not only was the pain eating him alive but so was the guilt. He should've told Julian when his knee had started hurting, but he was afraid the trainer would pull him off the equipment and send him back to Arkansas.

The sound of the shower curtain sliding open signalled a visitor. "All done?" a familiar voice asked.

Shit. Bobby had hoped he'd have a few moments alone to get himself together. He scrubbed his hands over his face and turned around. "Yep. Julian's a hardass, but he'll have me back in shape in no time."

Chet's frame filled the shower opening as he stared at Bobby. "He told me you were having some problems with your knee."

Fuck. "Yeah, but it's getting better all the time. I shouldn't have any problems by the time the season starts." Bobby held his breath, hoping Julian hadn't given Chet a full rundown of his injury.

"You should've told me," Chet grumbled.

"I didn't want you to worry. It'll be fine in a couple of weeks." Bobby tried to stand with his weight balanced evenly on both feet so as not to draw attention.

Chet's gaze zeroed in on Bobby's left knee. "Does it feel sturdy enough to take a hit?"

"Not quite, but it will." *Understatement of the year.*

Chet slowly looked his way up Bobby's body, stopping to stare at Bobby's flaccid cock. That more than anything should've given him away. Normally Bobby's cock would be fully hard at the first sound of Chet's voice, but even after seconds of Chet eating him alive with his eyes, nothing.

"Julian asked if we want to have dinner with him and Koby," Chet finally said.

"Sure, if you want to. Mind if I call Dane and invite him?"

"No, go ahead," he said after a brief pause. He took one last look at Bobby's limp dick and stepped out of the doorway. "I'll be in my office when you're done," he said, closing the curtain.

The moment he heard Chet's footsteps on the tile, Bobby dropped to the floor. He worked his hands over his swelling knee and willed it to return to normal as once again, the tears began to slide down his face. Was he being unfair by taking a scholarship that could've gone to a talented incoming freshman? Bobby knew the only reason he'd received the late scholarship was because of his name. There was no doubt the fund had been scraped empty to give him the money he needed.

With the compounding guilt, Bobby began to wonder if a degree was worth it. What kind of social worker would he be after the deceit he'd resorted to in order to become one in the first place.

* * * *

Chet walked into his office and shut the door. It was something he rarely did out of respect for his staff and players, but after Bobby's reaction to him in the shower, it was something he desperately needed. He'd finally taken Bobby into his bed and opened his heart and mind to the possibility of something more. Could it be possible that after only a few days together Bobby was already losing interest? Troubling memories of his mom drifted to the forefront.

A knock on the door brought him out of his thoughts. "Who is it?"

"The big bad wolf," Julian replied. Chet could imagine his best friend rolling his eyes as he said it.

"Come in."

Julian stepped into the office and made a big production out of shutting it. "Where's your 'Do Not Disturb' sign?"

"Fuck off." Chet usually enjoyed Julian's sense of humour, but he wasn't in the mood. "What do you need?"

"A million bucks and a blow job in the next five minutes. What do *you* need?"

Chet laid his palms flat on his desk and leant forward. "Not today, Julian."

Julian held up his hands. "Fine. Did you ask Bobby Ray about dinner?"

"Yeah, but he wants to ask Dane."

"So much for the double date idea."

Chet stared out the window for several moments. "Do you think it's possible he's losing interest?"

Julian jumped out of the chair like his ass was on fire. "Do I look like a damn woman?" He shook his head and headed for the door. "When you need to know how to cure jock itch or something else manly, give me a call, but leave me the hell out of your chick shit."

Julian opened the door and walked through, but before he shut it, he poked his head back in and smiled. "No way is he tired of you. The guy thinks you walk on water for fuck sake. Now grab your balls and let's go have dinner."

Despite his earlier annoyance with Julian, Chet appreciated the way Julian could change his mood within minutes. He balled up a piece of paper and threw it at his friend. "Get the fuck out, you jackass."

After Julian left, Chet opened his desk drawer and pulled out a small picture of Bobby that he'd cut out of a Sports Illustrated article. It didn't matter how many times he looked at the picture it always made him smile. Unlike the majority of the pictures of Bobby Ray out there, this one had been taken back home in Arkansas. In it Bobby held up a snapping turtle who'd stolen his bait while fishing. The goofy expression on Bobby's face was priceless and one that Chet never tired of.

"I'm ready," Bobby said, sticking his head in the door.

"Be right there." Chet put the framed picture back in his drawer. He hoped to one day see that expression in person instead of in a magazine photo.

* * * *

"Dane's here," Bobby announced, getting up from the table to go meet his roommate.

Chet watched Bobby cross the restaurant. He stopped in front of his friend and the two men talked for a brief moment before both disappearing down the hallway towards the restroom.

"What, they're so close all the sudden they have to hold hands while they pee?" Julian asked around a chuckle.

Uneasy, Chet rose from his chair. "I'll be right back."

As he made his way to the restroom, the hairs on the back of his neck stood on end. Dane jumped the moment Chet pushed open the door.

"Hey," Dane greeted. "We'll be out in a minute."

Chet looked past Dane to the closed stall door. He nudged Dane out of the way and knocked on the cold painted metal. "Everything okay?"

"Uhhh, yeah, I'm almost done."

Through the slight crack in the door, Chet could see Bobby wasn't even sitting on the toilet. Chet grabbed the top of the door and hoisted himself up until he could see over the stall. With his pants around his ankles, Bobby was in the middle of wrapping a cold pack around his knee. "Open the door."

Bobby glanced up at Chet and secured the Velcro firmly in place. "Hang on. Let me pull my jeans up."

Chet lowered himself to the floor and turned to Dane. "Would you mind joining the others while I have a word with Bobby?"

Dane, who'd been steadily working on biting his thumbnail off, glanced at the closed stall door. "Bobby?"

"It's okay," Bobby said, opening the door. He patted Dane on the shoulder and smiled. "Thanks for your help, but I've got it from here."

"You sure?" Dane asked.

"Yeah."

Although part of the conspiracy to deceive him, Chet had to give Dane points for loyalty. The two men had only known each other a few days and already they seemed like best friends.

"Don't be mad at Dane," Bobby started.

"I'm not." Chet leaned his back against the door and crossed his arms over his chest. "How bad are you hurtin'?"

Bobby bit his bottom lip and had the decency to look guilty. "Pretty bad, but I'm sure it's just because it's been a while since I've worked out like I did today."

Chet's biggest fear had come to fruition. Caught between being a coach and being a lover, he warred with himself on what to do. It was the first real test of their new relationship and he wanted to get it right.

"Why don't we go back to my house? I'll help you ice it down and we can talk."

"Are you mad?" Bobby asked.

"Some, but more than anything, I'm hurt that you went to Dane for help instead of coming to me." Bobby opened his mouth to protest, but Chet held his hand up. "I didn't say I don't understand why you did it, but maybe that's something else we should talk about."

Chet opened the door and wrapped a supportive arm around Bobby's waist. "By the way, you're going to have to deal with Julian. He won't be happy you pushed yourself so hard."

"I know."

"Do you? Because you haven't seen Julian mad. Believe me, it's not pretty."

"Just get me out of here, and I promise to deal with Julian tomorrow."

Once back at the table, Chet opened his wallet and signalled for the waitress. "Can we get these two plates put in to-go containers?"

After the waitress accepted Chet's money and took away the plates of food, Chet addressed Julian. "I think Bobby over did it today. I'm going to take him home and ice him down."

Julian narrowed his eyes and stared straight at Bobby. "Just sore or something worse?"

"Just sore, I think," Bobby said. "I'll be back in the training room in the morning, don't worry."

"Sorry about dinner," Bobby told Dane.

"It's okay. Will you be home tonight?" Dane asked.

"No," Chet answered.

Bobby elbowed Chet in the ribs. "I can answer a simple question for myself," he reminded Chet. "I'll catch up with you sometime tomorrow," he told Dane.

Chet took the takeout containers from the waitress and passed her back a tip. "Thanks."

"Call me in the morning if you're too sore to work out," Julian instructed.

"I won't be," Bobby threw over his shoulder as they left the restaurant.

"You won't be sore? Or you'll work out regardless?" Chet asked, helping Bobby into the SUV.

"I'll work out regardless. I've got a coach who'll be on my ass if I'm not in shape for practice on Thursday."

"And a boyfriend who'll make sure you don't do anything to cause serious damage to yourself." Chet was pleased with himself after that remark. Yeah, he could do this boyfriend-coach thing after all.

* * * *

Dane agreed to go with Bobby to BK House the following day after his workout. "Looks like you're still favouring your left leg," Dane said as he got out of his small silver Mercedes SLK.

"A little. Julian was pissed because of yesterday, so he got even today."

"He worked you that hard even though you were already sore?"

"No, just the opposite. He made me sit in an ice bath for an hour. I think I've lost all feeling from the waist down." Bobby walked into BK House like Locky had instructed. "You've been here before, right?"

Dane grinned. "I lived here for two years, but found it hard to study."

"Too noisy?" Bobby asked, heading towards the common room.

"No, too many people." Dane ducked his head. "I told you, I'm not comfortable around people."

Bobby wrapped his arm around Dane's neck and pulled him in to rub the top of his head. "I think you're great."

"I think you're pretty great, too," Dane mumbled, pushing Bobby away.

There were only two people in the large room, one playing pool and the other in front of the large television mounted on the wall.

"Is that Scatterbug Triple Threat?" Dane asked.

The guy playing looked up in surprise. "Yeah. It's not even in the stores yet. Mr Bianchi brought it over earlier. Wanna play?"

Dane looked at Bobby. "You mind?"

Bobby shoved Dane towards the couch. "Go play your stupid game, geek boy."

"You only say that because you've never played."

"Neither have you," Bobby fired back.

"You're right, but I'm about to." Dane jumped onto the couch with more enthusiasm than Bobby had seen from him outside of having his nose buried in that damn book he carried around all the time. *Go Dane.*

Bobby decided to introduce himself to the cute blond at the pool table. "Hey," he greeted. "I'm..."

"Bobby Ray Sikes," the guy finished for him. "I'm a big fan." The kid moved his pool stick to his left hand and stuck out his right. "I'm Chase Hughs, freshman quarterback from Cattle Valley, Wyoming."

"Good to meet you." Bobby was flattered the freshman player knew who he was. "Care to play a game?"

Chase's eyes opened wide. "You want to play with me?"

"I wouldn't have asked if I didn't."

Chase looked up at the large digital clock on the wall. "I'd love to, but it'll have to be a short one. I'm due at work in an hour."

"Work?"

"Yeah. Mr Bianchi gave me a full-time job cleaning offices after hours. It'll work perfectly once practice starts because as long as I get my work done before the place opens in the morning, I can pretty much set my own hours."

In the three years he'd played football at college level, Bobby had never heard of a player having a full-time job. "You on scholarship?"

"Partial. My tuition and part of my dorm fees are covered, but I still have to come up with money for books, food and..." Chase held his hands up and gestured around the room. "It's worth it though. I can't imagine living in the regular dorms."

"Take it from me. They suck." Bobby grabbed the rack off the peg on the wall and set up the table.

He spent the next thirty minutes getting his ass beat by Chase before the younger man had to quit to go to work. "Sorry, maybe next time we can play two out of three or something," Chase said on his way out of the door.

Bobby stared in the eighteen-year-old's direction long after he'd disappeared from sight. Chase had talked nonstop about his love of the game, and how excited he was to play for Coach Nelson and Coach Sloan. Bobby had hated to break it to the kid that Justin Nelson only helped with the team when he wasn't coaching the junior high kids.

Chase had laughed and simply said, "Duh. I've read everything written about Coach Nelson, but just the chance to have him give me a few tips here and there is worth it. And getting a scholarship was the only way it could happen."

"I hear ya," Bobby had said. "I'm a scholarship kid, too."

Bobby turned away from the door and rubbed his chest. Chase had the next four years in front of him. Maybe, if he was lucky, he'd get a full ride next year. Surely a guy of eighteen could survive on only a few hours of sleep a day, right? Yet another stone of guilt landed in Bobby's gut.

Chapter Five

Bobby went to the practice field early to watch the incoming freshmen go through drills before the rest of the team took the field. He'd been ordered to sit the first couple of practices out until Julian and Chet were confident his knee could handle the normal drills the team was put through.

He'd overheard Chet discussing the talented crop of players with Coach Nelson the previous day and wanted to see for himself how good they really were. It seemed Coach Nelson was more than just a nice guy. He was known around the conference as the Star Recruiter because he seemed to get the pick of the litter every year.

As Bobby watched the practice, his gaze landed on Chase Hughs, the quarterback he'd met a few days earlier. In the five minutes Bobby observed the enthusiastic player, Chase yawned three times. No wonder. Between conditioning, a full-time job and trying to adjust to life away from home, Chase had to be dead on his feet.

On the scooter he'd become known for, Coach Nelson drove to where Chase was tossing the ball with another player. Bobby smiled at the expression on Chase's face as Coach Nelson gave him a few tips. There was something in Chase that made Bobby uncomfortable and it suddenly dawned on him what it was. Chase not only played football, he seemed to live for it, love it. Bobby wouldn't be surprised if Chase ran through plays in his sleep. *Have I ever felt like that?*

He knew the answer as soon as he'd asked himself the question. No. He'd always enjoyed the game more because he seemed to take to it naturally than because he loved the game itself. His childhood hadn't been like most kids his age. Never had he been allowed to sit in front of the television and watch cartoons all day. If he didn't have chores to do, he was expected to be out of the house finding something that involved a ball to occupy his time.

It wasn't until he was in high school that he'd played his first video game at a friend's house. The only thing Bobby had been allowed to do that didn't involve a ball was fishing in the family pond. He'd loved his dad, but there were times he'd felt he was living his life for his dad rather than for himself.

Earl Sikes had been a star football player in high school, and he was bound and determined that his only child would be even better. His dream for Bobby Ray was to play his way through college, something Earl had never been quite good enough to do.

Watching Chase made Bobby feel like a fake. He spotted the more experienced players jogging towards the practice field and tried to push Chase from his mind.

After an hour of watching last year's team practice, Bobby couldn't take anymore. The junior running back, Colson Farley, was good—damn good. Bobby wondered what Colson thought of a senior dropping in to take his position. He stood and tried to sneak away without garnering Chet's attention. He managed to evade Chet's notice, but not Julian's.

"Bobby Ray, wait up," Julian called, running towards him.

Shit. Bobby stopped and shielded his eyes against the bright afternoon sun. "Hey."

Julian slowed to a stop when he reached Bobby. "Is everything okay? You're not hurtin' are you?"

Actually, he felt like he was dying, but he couldn't tell Julian that. "Just thirsty. Thought I'd go in for a bottle of water."

Julian's eyebrows drew together. "There's water right down there on the field."

"Yeah, for the players. I don't think I qualify today." Bobby turned and started moving towards the safety of the locker room.

"Why don't you soak your knee in the tub while you're in there," Julian suggested.

Bobby lifted his hand in acknowledgement and continued walking, trying his best not to limp. Once he stepped into the air conditioned facility he grabbed a bottle of water out of the fridge in the exercise room. As he drank, he stared at the VertiMax. He knew he wouldn't be well enough to play until he could gather the guts to work out on that damn thing.

Bobby put the bottle down, and began the process of setting up the tension bands on the machine. He found the belt draped over the nearby bench and fastened it around his waist. Finally clipped to the tension bands, Bobby took a deep breath. After counting down from three, Bobby attempted his first jump. Although not pretty, he managed to land the jump without crumpling to the ground. He tried again, this time using more force on his push-off. His left leg started to buckle on the landing, but he kept his footing. It seemed he'd reached his limit and he'd barely been able to get off the ground.

He tore off the belt and left it on the VertiMax still clipped to the tension bands. Bobby grabbed the bottle of water and finished it off on his way to Chet's office. He sat in one of the chairs in front of Chet's desk and slid the phone closer, punching in numbers without thought.

"Hello?"

"Hi, Mom." Bobby rested his forehead against the edge of the desk with the handset held in a white-knuckle grip.

"Is everything okay? You don't sound like yourself."

"Right now I don't even know who I am, so I don't doubt I sound different."

"You're talking in puzzles, Bobby Ray. Spit it out. What's going on?" Ellen asked.

"My knees not getting better. I had a plan before I left home, but now I don't think I can go through with it."

"You need that surgery, don't you?"

"Yeah. Either that or give up football." Bobby turned his head to the side and rested his cheek on the cool metal desktop.

"What does Chet say?"

Bobby bit his bottom lip. "I haven't told him. He thinks I'm getting better." He knew he had to tell his mom all of it or the guilt would eat him alive. "Here's the thing. All I have to do is step on that field in my first game and the scholarship is mine regardless, that's the deal I worked out with Coach Nelson. So, I figured, I'd fake my way through a couple of games and take my chances that the surgery would fix any damage I do."

"But..." Ellen prompted when Bobby didn't continue.

"I like these people. And I can't help but feel that I'm cheating my way through college."

"That's because in a way you are. I can't tell you what to do, Bobby Ray, but you know I can't send you any more money than I already do. Believe me, I wish I could, but it's just not there. That's why the scholarship is so important."

"I know." Chase's face kept popping up in his guilt-ridden mind. "I guess it's something I'll have to think about."

"I'm sorry that I can't do more for you, baby."

"Don't be sorry, Mom. I'm twenty-two. I should be able to figure this out on my own."

"You're still my baby, don't forget that. Call me anytime."

"I will. Thanks." Bobby hung up the phone and groaned in frustration. After talking to Chase, Bobby had sat down and figured out the cost of the credit hours he needed to graduate. They were more than he could pay for even with a good job. He was pretty sure Chet would let him live at his house, but that wasn't the way Bobby wanted to get there.

Leaning back in the chair, Bobby decided to play it day by day until the moment came when he couldn't take his decision back.

* * * *

"Chet?"

"I'm in here," Chet answered, putting the finishing touches on one of his most recent model aeroplanes.

Dressed only in a loosely-tied robe, Bobby stepped into the guest room and grinned. "What's that? Playing with toys on the sly?"

Chet held up the plane. "It's a Cessna 182 radio-controlled plane. I'm not sure I would consider it a toy. It took hours to complete and a hell of a lot of money."

Bobby separated his robe and straddled Chet's lap. "You can really fly that thing?"

"Sure, as long as I've put it together right." Chet slipped his hands inside the robe and ran his palms down Bobby's back. There was something so warm and peaceful about the man in his arms. Chet sighed and rested his forehead against Bobby's shoulder. While he knew he could seduce Bobby into going back to bed for a while, Chet found he rather liked just holding the man he'd fallen in love with.

"This is so cool. Why didn't I know you did this?"

Chet had come to realise in the last several weeks that he and Bobby actually knew very little about each other outside of football. It didn't diminish Chet's feelings in any way. On the contrary, Chet found it exciting to discover new sides to Bobby, and he hoped Bobby felt the same. "I hadn't worked on this one for a couple of months, but I found it while cleaning the garage the other day and decided to finish it. You want to go out to the airstrip with me to see if she flies?"

"Hell yeah," Bobby said.

Within minutes Chet had the plane loaded in the back of his SUV along with his trusty four channel radio. He grabbed a blanket out of the linen closet and a few supplies from the bedroom and they were ready. "I thought maybe we'd have a picnic. Ya know, make a day of it. Feel like stopping by the deli and picking up a couple of sandwiches on the way?"

Bobby reached over and tickled the skin on Chet's neck with his fingertips. "Sure, I guess, although I've never been to a picnic at the airport."

Chet laughed and reached over to squeeze Bobby's upper thigh. "We're not going to the airport. We're going to the airstrip. It's a big field out in the middle of nowhere with a small dirt track on it. Perfect for flying and privacy." He moved his hand further up Bobby's leg to brush the back of his hand against the front of Bobby's gym shorts. "I found it a couple of years ago and asked the owner if I could fly from it occasionally."

Bobby pushed his shorts down far enough for the head of his cock to peek out over the waistband. "I can take them off if you want?"

Chet brushed his thumb over the tip, gathering a drop of pre-cum, before sucking it into his mouth. It was hard enough to concentrate on driving with the taste of Bobby coating his tongue. No way could he function responsibly if his little sex machine was naked from the waist down. "Hold that thought until we get to the airstrip."

Chet pulled in front of a small deli he'd found soon after he'd arrived in town. "Coming or staying?"

Bobby glanced down at his hard cock. "What do you think?"

Laughing, Chet gave Bobby's cock one last squeeze before climbing out of the SUV. It was building up to be a fantastic Sunday afternoon.

* * * *

Naked, Bobby lay on his back and watched the aeroplane as it soared through the sky. Chet stood a few feet away, equally naked, with a huge smile plastered to his face. Bobby's gaze alternated between watching the tricks Chet was able to perform with his plane and watching the man who had captured his heart so long ago.

Lust for the like-minded man might have been what had initially driven him into Chet's arms, but Bobby knew his feelings had grown far beyond an eighteen-year-old's curiosity. For three years while playing football under another head coach, Bobby dreamed of someday playing for Chet. Now that he had the chance, Bobby wasn't sure he wanted it.

Chet made a noise of jubilation. "Did you see that one?"

Bobby looked away from Chet's half-hard cock to his face. "Nope. Sorry, I was distracted."

Chet took his attention off the plane and glanced down at Bobby. Within seconds, Chet's cock started to harden. "Give me a minute and we'll see what we can do about that distraction problem you seem to be having."

Bobby got to his feet. "I have another idea." He moved to kneel in front of Chet, the soft field grass cushioning his knees. With Chet still flying the plane, Bobby wrapped his hand around the base of Chet's cock and licked his way from root to crown. The sun-warmed skin felt heavenly against Bobby's tongue, but he craved the fluid forming at the slit.

Chet thrust his hips forward when Bobby enveloped the head of his cock with his mouth. "Shit. I gotta get this thing on the ground."

Bobby continued to work his way up and down Chet's length as Chet tried to land the plane safely.

The moment the plane was on the ground, Chet stepped back, pulling his cock free of Bobby's mouth. "Blanket," he growled.

Bobby wiped his mouth as Chet helped him stand. "I like it out here," he whispered against Chet's lips.

"Me, too." Without releasing his hold on Bobby, Chet walked them towards the blanket.

Bobby eased down and reached for the lube as Chet rolled on a condom. "Are you ever going to fuck me without one of those things?"

"Not until I'm sure," Chet answered.

"Sure of what? I'm clean. I've already told you that."

Chet shook his head and knelt between Bobby's legs. "It's not about being disease-free for me. It's about committing my heart one hundred per cent to one person. Unfortunately, in this state I can't legally marry that one special someone, but I can give him something no one else has ever had."

Although Chet's words were beautiful, it hurt Bobby to know Chet still didn't believe enough in him to know he was that one special person. "I can be that person for you."

Chet took the lube out of Bobby's hand and coated his fingers. "We'll have a better idea if that's true or not after football season's over."

Bobby was spread wide open with Chet's fingers working his asshole and still Chet looked at him as a player instead of an equal. Closing his eyes, Bobby tried to calm his racing heart. It was no use. His anger bubbled up and exploded.

"Damn you." Bobby pushed Chet and scrambled out from under him. He stood and grabbed his shorts and underwear.

"What the hell'd I do?" Chet asked, getting to his feet.

"Just take me home," Bobby said, stuffing his feet into his sneakers. He bent and picked up the sack of lunch trash and his shirt before heading to the SUV.

"Dammit, Bobby!" Chet yelled.

He opened the door and climbed into the passenger seat. The SUV was hotter than hell, but no way would he go back and ask Chet for the keys so he could roll down the windows. He mopped at his face with his T-shirt and stared straight ahead. The back of the vehicle opened and Chet set the plane inside before slamming the lift gate closed hard enough to make the entire SUV shake.

Bobby didn't even glance Chet's way when he got behind the wheel and fired up the engine. What good would it do to get into an argument? Bobby knew as long as he played ball, Chet would always see him as a player first and a boyfriend second. He'd been stupid to think he could have both.

Not a word was spoken on the drive home. Chet pulled into the garage, and Bobby immediately got out and headed for his pickup.

"That's it? You're not going to say anything?" Chet asked.

Bobby turned his head to the side to yell over his shoulder. "Yeah. Give me a call when football season's over."

* * * *

Bobby sat on the deep leather couch in the media room of Dane's house and stared at the piece of paper in his hand. It had been four days since he'd spoken to Chet. It seemed he wasn't the only one in the mood to avoid a potential fight. Chet had started passing basic coaching messages through Julian.

The answer to the most important of those messages was in Bobby's hand. He'd finally done it. He'd sold his soul and values to play one more year of football.

"How'd it go?" Dane asked, hopping over the back of the couch to sit beside Bobby.

Bobby passed him the sheet of paper. "It was a lot easier than I thought."

Dane whistled and set the paper on the end table. "How'd you get a doctor to sign off on it?"

"I told him about the partial tear but I lied about the dates. I told him I felt a hundred per cent better and my knee seemed to be stable enough for me to return to football. He examined me, made me pee in a cup and dallied with my balls while I coughed."

"That's it?"

"Not quite. He put me through a few exercises, but I've gotten so good at hiding the pain he had no idea."

Dane pushed his glasses up on his nose and made a disapproving noise. "Did you tell Coach Sloan?"

"Nope. I thought I'd put the release on his desk tomorrow before practice."

Dane wrapped his arms around Bobby's arm and hugged it, fitting his head on Bobby's shoulder. "I wish you'd go talk to him. You've been so miserable the last few days."

Bobby kissed the top of Dane's blond head. Even though Dane was older, Bobby couldn't help but think of the guy like a younger brother. Maybe it was Dane's naïve nature or the fact that even though he claimed to feel uncomfortable around people, he sure did like physical attention of any kind. Bobby often wondered if Dane received any affection at all when he was a child.

"Have you ever loved someone older?"

"Yeah," Dane whispered. "Why?"

"Because I'm trying like hell to figure out a way for Chet to see me as a man and not a player or a student."

Dane moved his head to rest his chin on Bobby's shoulder. "I don't know, but if you figure it out would you let me know?"

Bobby grinned and narrowed his eyes. "What're you keeping from me? You have a crush on someone?"

"No!" Dane tried to pull away, but Bobby saw the lie written all over his friend's face.

He held on tight and tried to go through everything he knew about Dane. Hell, the man never went out unless it was with him, so who could it be? He thought of the book Dane never seemed to be without. "Is it Professor Sofokleous?"

Dane sucked in a breath and gave up trying to fight Bobby off. He resettled his glasses and stared up at Bobby. "Promise me you won't say a word to anyone about that. No way am I in his league, and if he found out he'd never let me be his teaching assistant."

"I'll keep your secrets if you keep mine."

* * * *

In the early morning glow of the sun, Bobby finished warming up before turning to Dane. "Okay. The second I take off, start the stopwatch."

"Got it."

Bobby got to his feet and shook out his limbs, mindful of twisting his knee. He knew there was no way he could match his usual time of 4.32 in the forty, but he had to know just how off he was before practice. The last thing he wanted was to make a fool of himself in front of the players and coaching staff.

He eyed the finish line and got into position. "Ready?" he asked Dane without looking over.

"Yep."

Bobby took a deep calming breath before taking off. Each time his left foot hit the synthetic track, he prayed his leg wouldn't buckle under him. He gave the short forty yard dash everything he had but it cost him. After crossing the line, Bobby immediately slowed and made his way to the soft grass on the interior of the track.

He dropped to the ground, praying he hadn't done further damage to the ACL. "What was it?"

Dane took off his glasses and wiped his eyes before resettling them. Instead of announcing the results, Dane carried the stopwatch over and handed it to Bobby. "I think it's pretty accurate."

Bobby stared at the watch in disbelief. 5.29. He'd run a faster time than that in high school. Still, in the grand scheme of things, it was better than he'd thought it would be. Bobby looked up at Dane. "Could you tell?"

"That you were hurting? No."

Satisfied that he could participate in basic drills at practice, Bobby stood and took the bottle of water Dane held out. "I'm going to jog around once."

"Want some company or is this a thinking thing?"

Bless his friend for already understanding him. "Thanks, but it's one of those thinking things." He took off down the track at a slow jog. Truth be told, his knee was feeling much better. Given time, it could possibly heal without surgery. Unfortunately, using the knee in everyday life was nothing like the rigorous workout it would receive on the football field.

Bobby was halfway around the track when he thought of giving the doctor's release to Chet. He'd gone over their fight hundreds of times and realised he'd made more of Chet's statement than he should have. Of course Chet would see him as a player. Coaching was the man's profession, and Bobby Ray was his top recruit.

By the time he reached Dane again, he'd kicked his own ass several times. "Can I borrow your phone?"

Dane grinned and passed it over. "I'll be in the car."

"Thanks." Although it wasn't yet seven o'clock, Bobby hoped Chet would be awake.

"Dane? What's happened?" Chet answered, fear in his voice.

"It's not Dane, it's me."

"Are you okay?"

"No. Can I come by and talk to you?" Bobby hoped he hadn't screwed up what they'd started to build.

"Sure. I don't have to go in until ten."

Bobby heard the bedding rustle and wanted to tell Chet to stay where he was, but the problems they needed to work out couldn't be fixed with sex. "I'll have Dane drop me by if you can give me a lift back to the house before you go to work?"

"I can do that."

There was something in Chet's voice that made Bobby uneasy. Maybe Chet had already washed his hands of the whole situation. Bobby prayed that wasn't the case. "Okay. Thanks. I'll be there in ten minutes."

Bobby hung up the phone, feeling only slightly better than he had before the call. Football be damned. There were some things more important than a fucking game.

Chapter Six

By the time the doorbell rang, Chet was dressed and had a pot of coffee brewing. As he made his way to the door he realised he was more nervous than the night Bobby drove into town for the first time.

Opening the door, Chet's chest tightened. *Please don't tell me it's over.* He stepped back and gestured towards the kitchen. "Want a cup of coffee?"

"Sure." Bobby waved to Dane. His roommate gave him a thumb's up before pulling out of the driveway.

"Afraid I wouldn't let you in?" Chet asked, walking towards the kitchen.

"Something like that," Bobby mumbled after shutting the front door. "I know I overreacted, and I'm sorry."

The apology right off the bat surprised Chet. He stopped and turned to face Bobby. "It's a hard thing we're trying to do. I'm fourteen years older than you are, and I haven't managed to figure out how to do it." He wanted to pull Bobby into his arms and tell him it would be okay, but he knew they needed to talk. "Have a seat."

Bobby sat at the kitchen island while Chet filled two cups. He added sugar to both cups before sitting one in front of Bobby. "Your call surprised me. What're you doing up so early?"

Bobby fidgeted on the stool, finally taking a sip of the coffee before finally answering. "Dane was timing my forty yard dash."

"Really. And how did you do?"

"Not great, 5.29."

Bobby was right, 5.29 wasn't nearly what he'd been clocked at in the past. "What about the pain level? Do you think it's something you can build on?"

Bobby shrugged. "Without surgery? I don't know."

Chet opened his mouth to speak but nothing came out for several moments. "Surgery?" He narrowed his eyes at the star running back. "Exactly what's wrong with your knee?" He had a sneaking suspicion he knew, but he needed to hear it from Bobby.

"Partial ACL tear," Bobby mumbled. "But I went to a doctor yesterday and he signed a release. It's just gonna take me some time to see if I can build my speed back up."

Chet jumped up from the stool so fast he knocked it over. He ran his hands through his hair and began pacing the kitchen. "You didn't tell me."

"No, I didn't." Bobby had the good sense to look shamed. "I need to play. I need that scholarship if I'm going to get my degree."

Once again, Chet tried to separate his personal life from his career as a coach. The lie hurt more on a relationship level, but the news was devastating to the coach in him. "Do you know what'll happen if you reinjure it, or worse, tear it completely?"

"Yeah, I know." Bobby stood and righted Chet's fallen stool. "I may be a hell of a lot younger than you, but I still understand how getting drafted works. We both know my chances are slim either way at this point. Even if I were lucky enough to get picked, it'd be far down in the draft." Bobby shook his head. "That's not the way I want my life to go. I'd be a fool to take a small salary and still be expected to hide my sexuality."

"If you have the surgery now, there's still a chance you'll rehab and be well enough to show the scouts what you can do before the draft."

"But then I'd lose my scholarship." Bobby reached out and placed a hand on Chet's shoulder. "I want a real life with a real partner, and I can have that with a degree. In my opinion it's a much better choice than a lonely existence as a pro."

Chet couldn't believe what he was hearing. "You've worked your whole life to go pro. Why would you give up on that dream now?"

"Because it was never my dream, it was Dad's. I knew the first time Mom drug me with her into the food pantry in town so we'd have something to eat that I wanted to grow up and help people like my mom and dad." Bobby tugged on Chet's arm until Chet turned to face him. "You and that degree mean more to me than playing football."

Torn, Chet weighed the options. "Just live here, and I'll pay for your school then. That way you can have the surgery and still have a chance at the pros if you change your mind."

"No. It's not the way I was raised. Did you know that when my dad was laid off from his job he volunteered to paint the food pantry that was helping us get by? You know why he did it?"

"I have a pretty good idea." Chet had had a great deal of respect for Bobby's father.

"Because he said Sikes men always paid their debts, if not in money, then in hard work. I've never forgotten that. It's the reason I worked my ass off to get the scholarships. I may not be able to pay for college, but I can damn sure give something back if they're letting me go for free."

Chet respected Bobby's position, but he couldn't do nothing and take the chance he'd get seriously injured. "I have the money to pay for your school. Hell, pay me back after you graduate if it's so important to you."

Bobby's arms slipped around Chet's waist. "I've already let my dad down in so many ways. I just don't think I can do it again."

Chet enveloped Bobby in a hug and kissed his forehead. "If you really think your dad would rather you play hurt than take a loan from someone who loves you, you're wrong. He wanted nothing more than to see you succeed, but not at the risk of your health. Fathers aren't like that, and your dad was no different."

Bobby stepped out from Chet's embrace and looked him in the eyes. "If I have a release, will you let me play?"

"Am I answering as your coach?"

"Yes."

"You'll have to fight Colson Farley for the position."

Bobby nodded. "Okay. That's what I needed to know."

Bobby started to sit at the island once again, but Chet pulled him up short. "Now that football's out of the way, I think it's time we talk about what happened the other day." Bobby started to open his mouth, but

Chet stopped him with a finger against his lips. "And about the lies. Unfortunately, I have to be in a meeting in forty-five minutes. Why don't you come over for dinner later, and we'll hammer out what the hell went wrong."

"You mean I have to go all day feeling this way?"

Although Chet was still angry, his feelings for Bobby hadn't changed. "Will a kiss get you through the day?"

"Maybe. If it's a really good one," Bobby added with a grin.

Chet started slow, nibbling Bobby's bottom lip before seeking entrance. With a moan of acceptance, Bobby's lips parted and Chet's tongue teased its way inside. He eased his body closer and settled his hands on Bobby's ass, taking time to knead the twin globes through the thick nylon of Bobby's shorts. Damn, he wished he had more time before his meeting. He used his tongue to play with and tickle the inside of Bobby's mouth for several minutes before pulling back. "That damn mouth of yours is going to be the death of me," he panted.

"Naw, you're still too young to die. I know you think of yourself as an old man, but you haven't even reached your prime yet." Bobby touched the short hair at Chet's temple. "Do blonds turn grey?"

"Yeah, but the way I'm going, I'll lose my hair before it has a chance to turn."

Bobby grinned. "Actually, I like your gracefully receding hairline."

Chet chuckled and leaned in to nip Bobby's neck. "Thanks for noticing." He started to take a step back, but Bobby held on tighter.

"Your age has never bothered me, so why does it seem to bother you so much?"

Chet had never told Bobby about his parents, but maybe it was finally time. "My dad was twenty-seven years older than my mom."

"Really?"

"Yeah. Anyway Mom decided about eight months after I was born that she hadn't lived enough, so she left my sister and I with my dad and took off. Guess that's why I'm a little touchy about our age difference."

"That's bullshit. You don't actually think I'm gonna take off like your mom did, do you?"

Chet shrugged. "You've barely had time to stretch your wings. How do you know what you'll want five or ten years down the line?"

Bobby didn't jump right in with a comment like Chet had expected. Instead, he took several moments before answering. "I can understand why you'd worry, but I really don't think you need to. I mean, I don't have a crystal ball or anything, but I'm not the kind of person who enjoys going to bars and stuff. Even in Arizona I didn't really party with the other guys."

Everything Bobby said sounded too good to be true. Chet wondered if Bobby was simply telling him what he wanted to hear. Chet thought of the conversation he'd had with Julian. Was it possible Chet's past was the main obstacle in his relationship with Bobby?

"I don't think you give me enough credit," Bobby said. "I know I've done some things to let you down recently, but really all I want is a regular life."

"But you were meant for so much more than this," Chet tried to argue.

"No I wasn't. Like I told you, my fate was sealed the first time I went to the food pantry with Mom. I couldn't believe how many people were there that I knew." Bobby swallowed, enthusiasm for his chosen profession evident in his expression. "Good people, Chet. Men who worked with my dad stood in that line. I could see the shame in their eyes. They're the people I want to help, not some multi-billionaire playboy who's just after the fanfare that comes with owning a professional football team."

While Chet commended Bobby for his way of thinking, he was also afraid the young man was being too idealistic. "You're one person, babe. I'm not sure what you think you can accomplish but you could do a lot of good with the money the NFL would pay you."

"Why're you trying to talk me out of doing something I want to do?"

"I'm not. I just don't want you to settle for a normal life when you could do so much more."

Bobby stepped back, pulling out of Chet's arms. "I thought you'd understand."

"I'm trying to." Chet reached for Bobby but he took another step back.

"Will you still drop me by the house?" Bobby asked.

Chet knew he'd taken another step back in Bobby's eyes but wasn't sure what to do about it with only a few minutes before he'd have to leave. "Yeah. Let me get my bag."

* * * *

After a short warm-up in the exercise room, Bobby headed to the field for his first official practice. He still wasn't sure if he was doing the right thing, but he still had until the start of the first official game to make up his mind.

"You're practising for real?" Chase said, jogging towards him.

Chase's smile was infectious, and Bobby found himself grinning from ear to ear. "Thought I'd give it a go."

Chase settled in stride beside Bobby. "You mind if I walk with you?"

"Not at all."

Chase gestured towards a small group of players. "You met Farley yet?"

Bobby shook his head. "I've watched him, but I haven't met him. You?"

"Tried. He didn't seem interested in talking much after he found out I lived in BK. That's okay. My mom told me not everyone's intelligent or tolerant." Chase grinned.

"Your mom?"

"Yeah. Mom moved us to Cattle Valley when I was eight. It was right after I told her I was going to marry my best friend Sam. Sam's folks didn't take the announcement as well as Mom did. So she moved us from Ohio to Wyoming just so I'd never have to go through that again." Chase rolled his eyes. "Sounds totally stupid, I know, but that's the way my mom is. She's always put me first."

By the time Chase finished his long-winded explanation they were on the field. Chase stopped and dropped down on the thirty yard line. "Wanna warm-up with me?"

Bobby looked over towards the other players. He wasn't sure whether or not it was cool for him to work out with a freshman, but so far Chase had been the only player who'd approached him. "Sure."

He sat next to Chase and began stretching despite his earlier workout. A shadow fell over him and

Bobby glanced over his shoulder. "Hey," he said, staring up at his competition.

"Did the Prince finally decide to come down from his castle and play with us peasants?" Colson Farley asked.

Bobby couldn't blame Farley for the jab, he deserved it. "I've been healing from an injury, but I finally got my release, so here I am." He started to explain further, but Chase's earlier comment about the way Farley had treated him came to mind. Instead he returned his attention back to Chase. "Wanna run some sprints with me?"

Chase glanced from Farley back to Bobby with a satisfied smile. "Sure."

Bobby got to his feet and held out his hand to bring Chase up. They walked over to the track without looking back. Chase's low laugh sounded more like a giggle as he started a slow jog. "You're bad," Chase said.

"Naw, I'm just giving him back a little of what he gave you."

"Why?"

"What do you mean why?" Bobby readied himself for his first sprint. "I like you, kid." He took off as fast he could safely run, feeling good for the first time in a long time. Maybe his body was finally starting to heal properly.

Chase ran up on Bobby's side. "Give me all ya got," Chase said, pulling ahead.

Bobby bit the inside of his cheek and pushed himself to the limit. *Don't buckle*, he silently begged his injured knee. Twenty yards later he noticed Chet standing in the centre of the track with his arms crossed and an angry expression on his face.

Bobby slowed to a stop and walked the last several yards to stand in front of his coach. Despite his personal relationship with Chet, he knew it was important to show the man the proper respect in front of the team. "Coach."

Chet glanced at Chase. "Why don't you get with Coach Lange. I think he has a new play he wants to go over with you."

"Sure thing, Coach Sloan." Chase waved at Bobby. "Thanks."

Bobby nodded, knowing he was about to get an earful from Chet.

"What was all that about?" Chet asked.

"Nothing, just warming up with Chase."

Chet shook his head. "What'd you say to Farley?"

Bobby stared at Chet. Throwing Farley under the bus was out of the question. "He asked why I was suddenly practicing, and I told him I've just been released from an injury. Why?"

"He's pissed. I'm just trying to figure out why. I'm also trying to figure out what the hell you're doing racing Chase. Are you trying to push your body to another injury, or are you so wrapped up in impressing Chase that you've lost your mind?"

Bobby was guilty of running to impress but it wasn't Chase he needed to prove something to. It had been a stupid move and he knew it. "You want me to go smooth things over with Farley?"

"Yeah." Chet's voice dropped. "Although he's a good enough kid, he likes to talk. The last thing you need is someone spreading rumours about you."

"Right." Bobby gave his coach a nod before crossing the track to the field. He found Farley and waited until he was by himself before approaching. "Hey," he said, announcing himself. "I just want you to know I'm not here to steal your position. I just want the chance to play."

Colson snorted. "Yeah, right. Not only are you Bobby Ray Sikes but everyone knows you're fucking the coach. How confident would you be if you were in my position?"

It was the first time someone on the team had mentioned his relationship with the coach. Were the players talking about Chet behind his back? Bobby wanted to jump in to defend the man he loved, but he knew it would only make the situation worse.

Unsure of what to say, Bobby shrugged. "Forget it. I was just trying to smooth things over so we didn't butt heads all season."

When Farley just continued staring at him, Bobby turned and walked away. He couldn't care less if the asshole liked him, but disrespecting Chet was something else. Bobby jogged over to Peter Lange, the offensive coach who was currently running drills, and fell into line. He may not be able to outrun Colson Farley, but he'd still give each practice everything he had.

* * * *

Chet looked for Bobby after practice but he was nowhere to be found. He knocked on Julian's door and stuck his head in. "Have you seen Bobby?"

"Yeah. He told me to tell you he'd meet you at your place." Julian stood and grabbed his gym bag.

"Thanks."

Chet started to leave when Julian stopped him. "There's already some bad blood between Bobby Ray and Farley."

"Yeah, I kinda noticed. I'll talk to Bobby about it this evening." Chet hated to do it, but Bobby needed to understand he was the new guy.

"Yo," Julian said, calling Chet back once again.

"What?"

"From what I could tell earlier, the issue's Farley's to get over, not Bobby Ray's."

"What do you mean? What issue?" Chet asked.

"Farley knows about the two of you. I heard him talking shit in the locker room earlier. I shut it down, but it'll no doubt start up again."

"Thanks." No wonder Bobby hadn't stayed around to wait for Chet. He went back into his office and shouldered his duffle before heading out to his SUV. He noticed Farley in the parking lot talking to a few of the other players. It took a lot of willpower to get into his vehicle without causing a scene. "Shit," he mumbled once he'd closed the SUV door. One of his jobs as a coach was to make sure his players were a team on and off the field. The bad blood already brewing between Bobby and Farley could mean trouble if it wasn't nipped in the bud. Unfortunately, it sounded like Farley was in the wrong in this particular situation, but if he tried to talk to the junior running back it would no doubt come off like he was playing favourites.

Chet pulled out of the parking lot and headed towards home. He'd known from the start dating a player would land him in hot water, so why the hell was he surprised the water was already starting to heat up?

* * * *

Chet took the hamburgers off the grill and slid them onto buns before carrying the platter to the outdoor table. "Come and sit down," he told Bobby.

Bobby turned off the hose he'd been using to water Chet's flowers and joined him. The scene was so incredibly domestic it warmed Chet's heart. He watched Bobby pull out a chair and sit down, watching every move. Why couldn't a future with Bobby be easy?

Bobby cleared his throat. "Are you mad at me?"

"No," Chet said honestly. "I was just thinking about how good — natural — it felt to have you here like this."

"It's everything I've ever wanted," Bobby whispered.

Chet picked up his burger and took a bite. He gestured to Bobby's hamburger which was still sitting untouched. "Eat up."

Bobby pushed his plate towards the centre of the table and leant his muscled forearms on the mosaic top. "If something was to happen, and I lost my scholarship, could the money go to Chase?"

"Why Chase? What's going on between the two of you?" he asked, jealousy getting the better of him.

"Nothing outside friendship. I've watched him, and I can tell you he's better than Koby. But he's working a full-time job and trying to practice. Soon he'll also have classes to worry about. How long do you think he'll be able to keep it up? He's the one who has the ability to go pro. He loves the game like I never have. He's the one I'd pin my hopes on if I were you."

"You make it sound like I want you to go pro for me, but that's not the case. I just don't want you to give something up because you're afraid of it."

"Afraid?" Bobby sighed and reached for Chet's hand. "There are only two things I'm afraid of — losing you and not graduating. If I can somehow manage to accomplish those two things I'll have achieved everything I've dreamed of. Football is just a way to get what I really want out of life."

"Have you checked into financial aid?" Chet couldn't believe he was having this conversation. He should push Bobby to play football. *I'm a coach, dammit!* He tried to remind himself.

"It's possible I could get something next semester, but only because of my mom's financial situation. Although I do okay in grades, they aren't near enough to get me an academic scholarship."

"I don't think you should quit football, but I can't make that choice for you," Chet tried to explain.

"I know. My knee felt pretty good today. Maybe I'll be okay."

It was the discussion he'd been avoiding since learning the truth of Bobby's injury. "Will it change things between us if I decide to play Farley instead of you for the first few games?"

"No. As long as you make the decision based on performance, how can I argue with that?"

"Well, since we're on the subject, Julian told me Farley knows about us."

"It's not just Farely, Chet. That's what has me worried."

"I thought you didn't have a problem with people knowing you're gay." Was Bobby starting rethink coming out?

"I don't, but I have a problem with him talking smack on you because of me."

Chet threaded his fingers through Bobby's. "You let me worry about that, okay? I need you to concentrate on building up your speed. Your times are way off."

"I know. I'm gonna start running every morning with Dane and Chase until classes start. After that it'll just be me and Chase because Dane has to go in early to kiss Professor Sofokleous' ass or something."

Mention of Magnus Sofokleous made Chet uneasy. Although gorgeous beyond compare, Magnus wasn't the easiest man to get along with, even in bed. "Guess I didn't realise Dane studied under Magnus."

Bobby chuckled. "Dane'd love to do anything under Professor Sofokleous, but he's just working for him this year." His face turned bright red. "Shit, promise me you won't tell anyone what I just said. Dane would kill me if he knew I told."

"I won't tell anyone, but it might be a good idea to try and subtly steer Dane in a different direction. Magnus isn't someone Dane should mess with."

"Why? What've you heard about him?" Bobby asked.

Telling tales wasn't something Chet was comfortable with, especially when he had firsthand knowledge. "You gonna eat or not?" He picked up his own half-eaten burger and took a bite.

"Are we done talking?"

"For tonight. I'd just like to eat my dinner in peace and curl up on the couch with you for the rest of the evening."

"I'm game." Bobby smiled and pulled his plate back in front of him.

Chet realised they hadn't even discussed the fact that Bobby had kept his injury from him. As he chewed his food, Chet wondered if it was worth talking about. Nothing he could say would change what Bobby had done or why he'd felt he had to do it. Once again it went back to the blurred lines between player and boyfriend.

As he reached for the store-bought potato salad, Chet decided to let it go. There were more important obstacles for the two of them to overcome if they were going to make a relationship work.

Chapter Seven

Bobby couldn't believe the size of the crowd standing in line to get into the stadium. His stomach dropped when he saw more than one fan wearing a red and grey jersey with number thirty-two on the front and back, his number. Although Chet had broken the news to him the previous night, Bobby hadn't been upset about not starting until the moment he'd spotted those damn jerseys.

"You just get here?" Chase asked, banging on the hood of Bobby's truck with his fist.

"Yeah." He'd come to a conclusion earlier in the day that would probably change the way Chase thought about him. "You're kinda early."

Chase grinned. "Are you kidding? This is the first game of my college career."

"You know you probably won't see any game time, right?"

Chase rolled his eyes and leaned on the car door next to Bobby. "Of course I know that, but it doesn't make it any less exciting."

There. That sparkle in Chase's eyes said it all. Bobby knew for a fact he'd never felt like that. It made what he had to say that much harder. "You got a few minutes?"

"Sure."

Bobby swallowed around the lump in his throat. "I'm not going to play."

"What?" Chase chuckled. "Of course you are. The way you've been training lately, you're going to run circles around Farley in no time."

Bobby shook his head. "I'm not getting any faster, and I know I won't unless I have ACL surgery." He took a deep breath. "I came to tell Chet I'm quitting the team, but he's probably gonna be pissed because I waited so late to tell him."

"Why did you? Wait, I mean."

"Because I kept thinking I'd change my mind, but the game's in an hour, and I know I'm doing the right thing." He'd spent the entire day going over his options. Dane had been there when he'd finally come to the realisation that playing while injured was not only bound to snap his ACL entirely but hurt Chet in the process. Not to mention it would mean taking a scholarship he knew he couldn't earn honestly.

"You want me to come with you while you tell Coach?" Chase asked.

Bobby stuck his arm out the window and squeezed Chase's shoulder. "Thanks, but this is something I need to handle."

Chase nodded and took a step back. "Well you'd better get to it then."

Bobby couldn't leave his new friend without knowing. "Are you disappointed in me, too?"

"No. You know your body better than anyone. Doesn't mean you're going to stop talking to me, does it?"

"Of course not."

"Then do what you need to do. I'll have your back if anyone tries to talk shit on you."

Bobby chuckled. He could only imagine Chase going up against some of the defensive linemen. He opened the truck door and got out. Standing, his knee felt almost as good as new, but standing wasn't the issue. "Why do I feel like I'm getting ready to face the executioner?"

"Because you care about what Coach'll think." Chase bumped his shoulder against Bobby's. "Because you loooove him."

"Yes I do," Bobby agreed.

* * * *

Chet was in the middle of a pre-game coaches meeting when a knock sounded at the door. He glanced away from the whiteboard towards the door. "Julian, can you see who's out there and tell them I'm in the middle of a meeting."

"Sure thing." Julian stood and made his way to the door.

Chet turned back to the white board and finished diagramming the offensive play the team had been practicing.

"Coach. It's Bobby. He said he'd like to come in and talk to all of us," Julian announced.

Dammit. Chet knew Bobby had taken the news that he wouldn't start too easily. As much as he'd rather have a private conversation with the running back, he had a feeling it would be better for his career if he allowed Bobby to address the rest of the coaching staff as well. "Okay, let him in."

Bobby came into the room and shut the door. "Sorry to interrupt."

Chet felt like all eyes were on him, but when he looked at his staff he found Bobby held their attention. "What is it?" he finally asked.

Bobby swallowed several times, clearly nervous about something. "I'm not sure how many of you know this, but I've been struggling to come back from a partially torn ACL. I thought with physical therapy and training, I'd be able to heal enough to play out the season, but I don't think that's going to happen."

Chet's heart sank. "Just because you're not starting this first game doesn't mean we don't have faith that your speed will come back."

"I know, and I thank all of you for believing in me to that extent. But I know my body. If it hasn't come back by now, it won't. Not without surgery, anyway."

"So you're planning to have the surgery?" Julian asked.

"Yeah. As soon as I can get it cleared through insurance and get it scheduled." Bobby looked at Chet. "I'm sorry. I feel like I'm letting you down, but it's the right thing to do. There's no way I'd last the season with my knee the way it is, and I can't live with taking scholarship money that I can't earn."

As a coach, Chet was devastated by the news he'd lose out on the chance to coach one of the finest running backs to ever play college football, but as a boyfriend, he couldn't have been more proud of Bobby's decision. Chet knew his next question would put Bobby on the spot, but he needed one more answer. "You don't plan to drop out of school, do you?"

Bobby shook his head. "Not at all. I'll figure the financial stuff out. Like my dad used to say, work for what you get and your life will be richer for it."

Peter, the offensive coach finally spoke up. "Your times may be off what they used to be, but you're still a lot faster than a lot of the running backs in the nation."

"Maybe, but Farley's faster. He's earned the right to play."

Peter stood and held out his hand. "There're going to be a lot of disappointed fans out there, but I respect your decision. You have more than college ball to worry about. Do what you need to do to make sure you're fast enough for the pros."

Although Bobby didn't contradict Peter, Chet knew in his heart Bobby had no plans to go pro. Again, while it was a tough blow for the coach in him, it was a moment of jubilation for him personally. A quick check of the time told Chet they were due on the field. "We'd better get out there. I'll go talk to Reggie to see how he wants to handle the press."

The coaches stood and began to file out of the office. "Bobby, can I speak to you for a second?"

Bobby stopped and moved to the side to let the others pass. The moment they were alone, Chet shut the door and pulled Bobby into his arms. "You sure about this?"

Bobby nodded. "Like I told them, it's the right thing to do."

"And school?"

"Dane said I could mooch off him if I did the cleaning. He hates having outsiders come into the house every week, so it works out for both of us."

"And tuition?" Chet dared ask.

"Someone who cares a great deal for me offered to loan me money until I can apply for financial aid next semester." Bobby leaned in and kissed Chet. "That is if the offer's still good?"

"You know it is, but what made you change your mind?"

"I realised that stupid bull-headed pride I had going didn't mean much while I continued to lie to myself and you about my true condition. Just promise me one thing?"

"Anything," Chet said without reservation.

"See what you can do to get Chase some of my scholarship money."

"I can't promise anything. It's really not my decision, but I'll make the suggestion to the scholarship committee."

"That's all I ask." Bobby leaned in for another kiss, this one deeper. He thoroughly inspected the inside of Chet's mouth before breaking the kiss. "Now go out there and win one for Bobby Ray."

Chet rolled his eyes. "Bobby Ray had better have his ass somewhere watching."

"I wouldn't miss it for the world."

* * * *

Chet groaned. Having Bobby naked and under him was even better than winning his first game of the season. He continued kissing his way down Bobby's body and stopped when the head of Bobby's cock pressed against his chin. He looked up and stared into Bobby's eyes. For the first time since he'd first realised it, Chet didn't have any reservations about telling Bobby exactly how he felt. "I love you."

Bobby thrust his hips, sliding his cock over Chet's chin to brush his lips. "I know. Just like I hope you know how much I love you."

"I'm starting to," Chet replied before capturing Bobby's cock with his mouth. He pressed the underside of the spongy tip with his tongue as he suckled the head. Bobby squirmed under him, making noises that were quickly turning Chet on even more. He worked Bobby's cock as far down his throat as he could without gagging and grazed the sensitive skin with his teeth.

"Awww, fuck," Bobby moaned. "Fingers. I need fingers."

Chet chuckled at the commanding voice and nearly choked himself. He grabbed the base of Bobby's dick and eased his mouth back up its length before releasing it. "Where's the lube?"

Bobby handed Chet the bottle and a foil packet. Chet stared at the condom for several moments before opening it. As much as he wanted to fuck Bobby without it, Chet needed more time to be sure Bobby was the real deal. There were so many changes going on in Bobby's life, Chet needed more security than one day, one important decision to make that leap to forever.

He moved to his back and rolled the condom down his length before coating his fingers with lube. After insinuating his hand between Bobby's legs, Chet circled the wrinkled hole with the tip of his middle finger. "Feel good?"

"You know it does. I love it when you play with my ass."

Chet inserted his finger to the second knuckle. It amazed him how much freer he felt with Bobby now that he didn't have to worry about straddling that line between coach and lover. Bobby was his and only his, and Chet's job was to love and care for him. He slowly pushed in his ring finger, watching for any sign of discomfort.

With his head tilted to the side, Bobby stared at Chet with nothing but love in his eyes. "You're so beautiful," Chet whispered.

"And so ready for that cock of yours," Bobby shot back.

Laughing, Chet withdrew his fingers and rolled on top of the man he loved. Before he could reach between them to guide his cock to Bobby's stretched hole, the head of Chet's dick found it on its own. Evidently Chet's cock knew exactly where it wanted to be.

Chet rose up on his arms and pushed the crown of his cock past the ring of muscles to the warmth inside. "Ohhh," Chet moaned, as Bobby's body tightened around his length.

When Bobby moved one of his legs to drape over Chet's shoulder, Chet shook his head. "You'll hurt yourself."

Bobby shook his head. "No I won't. And even if I do, I promise not to tell the surgeon how it happened."

"Well in that case..." Chet positioned Bobby's other leg over his shoulder. Despite what he said, he took extra care to make sure he didn't twist the leg as he did it. Satisfied, Chet pushed the entire length of his cock inside Bobby.

Bobby began to squirm almost immediately, indicating his desire for more. Chet withdrew a few inches before surging back inside.

"Harder."

Chet repeated the movement, giving Bobby what he'd asked for. He'd never thought himself as a particularly good lover, but Bobby always made him feel like he could do no wrong, in bed anyway. There was something special about the way Bobby's head thrashed from side to side once Chet picked up speed that always threatened to send Chet over the edge.

"You like that cock fucking you?" Chet asked, slamming in once again.

"I love it," Bobby panted.

"You gonna fuck me someday?" Chet surprised himself by asking.

Bobby stilled. "Really?"

Chet stared deep into Bobby's eyes and nodded. "If you want to."

"I do. Someday." Bobby grabbed Chet's hips and prompted him to move. "But not today."

"Do that thing I like to watch you do."

When Bobby reached between them, Chet finally broke eye contact and looked down. The sight of Bobby jacking off never got old. He wondered if it made him some kind of pervert but realised he didn't care.

"So pretty," Chet groaned, picking up speed.

"Chet!" Bobby called out as the first strand of cum shot from his cock.

Chet grit his teeth as Bobby's body contracted around his cock. With a loud roar, Chet shot his seed into the condom, wishing like hell he didn't have the thin latex between them. He slipped Bobby's legs from his shoulders and carefully helped them to the mattress below before collapsing on top of the man he loved.

As he struggled to regain his breath, Chet prayed the day would come when he could envision a real future between them without doubts. Until that day, however, he'd soak up whatever love Bobby was willing to give.

* * * *

Chet was putting away the last of the dinner dishes when Ellen came into the kitchen. "Get it taken care of?"

Ellen shook her head and took the plate out of his hand. "No. He's being a pain in the neck this evening. Said if he needs washing you can do it."

Embarrassed, Chet searched for something to say. Ellen had arrived four days earlier, the day before Bobby's surgery, and since then Bobby had allowed his mom to do very little for him. "I'm sorry."

Ellen smiled and reached for Chet's hand. "Don't be. I knew this day would come the moment he told me he was transferring here."

That old feeling of guilt began to settle into Chet's chest. "Does our relationship bother you?"

"Of course not. He's happier than I've ever seen him."

That surprised Chet. Bobby had had only one evening to entertain his mom before he'd gone into surgery, and since the procedure he'd been a bear to everyone. "I think there must be something wrong with your happy metre because I know he's bitten your head off at least as many times as he has mine."

Ellen lifted Chet's hand to her mouth and kissed it before releasing him. "No offence, sweetie, but you haven't been around him the last few years." Ellen took a glass out of the cabinet and poured a glass of the wine leftover from dinner. "Bob was a good man, but he was especially hard on Bobby Ray. After Bob's death, Bobby Ray was finally able to live his life for himself instead of for his father." Ellen took a sip of her wine and watched Chet over the rim. "He may be as stubborn as his dad, but Bobby Ray has definite ideas of what he wants out of life, and if those things are here in Idaho, who am I to judge?"

"But he's so talented," Chet started to argue.

"Yes, he is, but football is only one of Bobby Ray's special gifts." Ellen shook her head. "He's been pushed enough in life. It's time for him to take the lead in where he goes from here."

Chet grinned. "Is that your way of telling me to back off about going pro?"

"Yes. How'd I do?"

"You were perfect, subtle but to the point."

"Excellent." Ellen refilled her glass. "Mind if I take this to my room?"

"Not at all." Chet leant over and kissed Ellen on the cheek. "Thank you for not hating me."

Ellen's eyebrows rose. "I did for a while after you left Arizona, but it was because you walked away from my son, not because you loved him." Ellen winked and left the room.

Although he wished he'd have done things differently, Chet didn't regret quitting his job in Arizona. Falling into a relationship with Bobby would've been too easy, and Chet had no doubt he'd have ended up pushing Bobby as hard as his father had. Their years apart had helped Bobby grow into the man Chet had come to love. The thought of Bobby growing to resent him for pushing was the last thing Chet wanted.

Chet walked into the bedroom with new resolve.

Epilogue

Bobby stretched his arms over his head before turning to watch Chet sleep. Weekends were usually the only time during the week he slept over, and although he didn't begrudge Chet his job, Bobby couldn't wait for the season to come to an end. Selfish or not, he could hardly wait for an entire weekend of Chet's undivided attention.

Bobby pressed his nose against Chet's warm chest and inhaled. Although faint, Bobby detected the smell of dried sweat and cum from their earlier lovemaking.

"Do I stink?" Chet asked, threading his fingers through Bobby's hair.

"Just the opposite." Bobby snuggled closer and rested his head on Chet's pillow. "Does my breath stink?"

Chet grinned and rolled over on top of Bobby. "Just the opposite."

"Liar," Bobby said around a chuckle. He opened his mouth to Chet's probing tongue and settled in for a long, leisurely kiss. When Chet tickled the roof of

Bobby's mouth with the tip of his tongue, Bobby couldn't hold back a laugh. He pulled away and shook his head. "I'm trying to be romantic."

"And I'm trying to get you to lighten up. You've had one hell of a week, and it's nice to hear that laugh I've come to depend on." Chet ground his morning erection against Bobby's. "I like it waking up with you in my arms."

"I like it, too." Bobby separated his legs, allowing Chet to get even closer.

"So stop being so stubborn and move in."

"I will eventually," Bobby said for the hundredth time.

"When? What the hell are you waiting on?" Chet asked.

"The time to be right," Bobby answered simply. Although he had no doubts about his feelings for Chet, Bobby wanted the same level of commitment before they took the next step. Childish or not, he needed the one thing Chet had yet to give, the ultimate promise.

Bobby smoothed his hands down Chet's back to land on his ass. He'd first fucked Chet two weeks earlier and had loved the way it felt to give Chet something so few had. Bobby's fingers slid down the crack of Chet's ass and whispered across his hole.

"Mmm," Chet moaned. "You gonna fuck me this morning?"

"Yep." Bobby tickled Chet's hole for several moments before stretching his arm out towards the bedside table. "I can't reach the stuff."

Chet dived for the drawer and slid it open. It took a few seconds but he eventually came back with the bottle of lube. Instead of passing it to Bobby, Chet held the bottle behind him and dripped a good stream of the slippery stuff down the crack of his ass.

"You're going to have to wash the sheets again," Bobby remarked when he felt the lube drip from Chet's ass to his sac.

"Don't care," Chet groaned when Bobby inserted the tip of his finger.

Bobby ran two other fingers through the lube and eventually worked them into Chet's hole. Chet rode Bobby's hand like he'd bottomed for years. It was Chet's reaction more than anything that prompted Bobby to top more than he'd probably like to. "Feel good?" he asked, brushing Chet's prostate.

Chet nodded enthusiastically and reached back to slap at Bobby's hand. "Fuck me already."

"Hand me a condom."

Chet stilled and stared down at Bobby. "No."

"Excuse me?" Had Bobby heard him right?

"No rubbers. Never again," Chet announced.

It was the announcement Bobby had waited months to hear. He wasn't about to question Chet on why he'd suddenly made the decision when they'd used a condom only hours earlier. "I'd like that."

Chet moved to straddle Bobby's hips. "So would I. Very much," he added.

Bobby squirted a few drops of lube onto his palm and greased his erection before holding it at the root. He stared into Chet's eyes as the man he loved slowly lowered himself on Bobby's length. It was one of those moments in his life he knew he'd never forget.

More than the feel of flesh on flesh, it was the trusting expression on Chet's face that said what words never could. Bobby swallowed around the lump of emotion lodged in his throat as Chet took his entire length.

"Stay with me forever," Chet whispered, before starting a slow rhythm up and down Bobby's cock.

"Okay," Bobby agreed. He had no doubt the moment was more intimate than any wedding ceremony ever performed.

Chet reached down and removed one of Bobby's hands from his hip. He lifted the hand to his lips and kissed each of Bobby's fingers before turning it over to kiss the palm. "You're my everything."

Moisture clouded Bobby's vision at the sentiment. He quickly blinked away the tears before they had a chance to fall. Instead of crying like a damn baby, Bobby thrust up to meet Chet's downward slide, driving his cock in hard.

Chet grinned, obviously getting Bobby's message. He released Bobby's wrist and braced his hands against Bobby's chest as he picked up speed.

Bobby wrapped his hand around Chet's cock. Although Chet loved to watch Bobby jack himself off, Bobby loved the control he felt making Chet come.

Chet's back arched as he came, impaling himself once more on Bobby's cock. "Fuck!" Chet howled as his body shook with the intensity of his climax.

The sight of Chet at the moment of release was enough to push Bobby over the edge. For the first time in their relationship, Bobby shot seed deep inside the man he loved. He couldn't wait to receive the same treatment from Chet. Although he might have to wait a few hours until after the last football game of the season, Bobby had no doubt he'd get his own brand of baptism before the day was through.

* * * *

Bobby pulled his baseball cap lower on his forehead as he made his way through the crowd towards the grandstand. Although most of the fans had understood his decision to quit football, there were still a few who enjoyed heckling him. If it weren't for Chet, Bobby doubted he'd have put himself through the torture, but after the morning they'd spent together, Bobby would do anything to make Chet happy.

He spotted a group of friendly faces and made his way to the section in front of the announcer's box. "Hey. Is that seat taken?" he asked Luc Henley, Coach Nelson's partner.

"It is now," Luc said, scooting over.

Bobby sat down between Luc and Tony Bianchi, nodding his thanks to both men before turning around to thump Dane on the leg. "I'm surprised to see you here."

Dane shrugged. "After that article they printed in the campus paper, I figured you could use all the support you could get."

Bobby squeezed Dane's calf. If he could've pulled the man into a hug he would have, but there were too many eyes on him. He felt each stare like it was a hot poker burning a hole into his body. Not only had he given up college football, but he'd announced in an interview with the school paper that he had no plans to enter the draft. His life was right on track as far as he was concerned, and although he still enjoyed watching football on television, Bobby had no desire to live a lifestyle that wasn't for him.

"I appreciate it," he told Dane before turning around. His gaze zeroed in on Chet only to find the love of his life staring back at him. Chet nodded before turning back to his players who were busy warming up on the field.

"It's good that you came," Luc said.

"Yeah," Bobby agreed. "Chet likes it when I do." He realised too late what he'd said. "I mean..."

Luc chuckled. "I know what you meant. But that wasn't why I said it. You may feel uncomfortable right now, but your attendance will go a long way in proving to the naysayers you're ready to stand by and defend the decision you've made."

Bobby shrugged. He wasn't out to prove anything to anyone except himself and Chet. "Let them say what they want. I know who I am, and what's right for me."

"Then you're miles ahead of a lot of these folks."

When the announcer asked everyone to stand for the national anthem, Bobby stood a little straighter than he ever had before. His life may not be perfect, but it was his, and he didn't plan to waste a moment of it.

A LESSON
LEARNED

Chapter One

Dane Jefferson stared at the sheet of paper in front of him and chewed the skin around his thumbnail. For two hours he'd contemplated his actions but wasn't any closer to reaching a decision.

Giving up, he reached for the phone. Although he was glad his best friend had finally agreed to move in with Chet, Dane missed having Bobby in the house.

"Hey," Bobby answered.

"Busy?" Dane asked.

"Just studying, but I could use a break. What's up?"

"Well, you know I need more hours of field experience..." Dane trailed off.

"Yeah."

"How wrong would it be if I sponsored something on my own but didn't tell Professor Sofokleous the grant was coming from me?"

"What're you up to, Dane?" Bobby asked, his voice thick with suspicion.

"I'm sitting here with a grant request form in my hands from Professor Sofokleous."

"He sent that to you?"

"No, he sent it to the James D Barrett Preservation and Historical Research Institute."

"So why do you have it?" Bobby asked.

"Because James Barrett is a distant grandfather. It's because of him that I became interested in anthropology in the first place. After I found and read Professor Sofokleous' book, I knew I had to study under him. Anyway, Mom gave me the request at Thanksgiving. She said it was something I'd be better suited to decide."

"So what's your dilemma?"

"Professor Sofokleous doesn't know I'm connected to the Institute, and since I want to be the one to accompany him on the research project I'd probably have to tell him. But will that make him even more uncomfortable around me than he already is?" Dane sighed. "I don't know what to do."

"How does the grant application look? Is it something you would approve even if you didn't want to sleep with him?"

"I honestly don't know. He's not asking for much money, but he wants to stay at Barrett House, something to do with getting answers to an unsolved mystery." Although letting visiting researchers stay at the house wasn't unheard of, Dane was uneasy. What mystery could possibly surround Barrett House? His ancestors had never owned slaves, so it had to be something involving Native Americans, Professor Sofokleous' area of study.

"Whatever you do, promise you'll be honest with him. You had a front row seat to the shit I stirred up with Chet when I tried to keep the truth from him."

"Yeah," Dane agreed. "But only if I approve the grant." He tried to imagine spending three weeks alone with Magnus Sofokleous. *Shit*. What if Magnus wanted to take someone else to assist him? "Would I be a complete loser if I insist he takes me with him as a condition of getting the grant?"

"Umm...yes, affirmative on that." Bobby chuckled. "Just go in and tell him the truth. If you want to go with him, state your case. He's an intelligent man. Surely he'll understand why you're interested."

Dane pushed his glasses up to rest on his short blond hair before rubbing his eyes. "Even though I know you're right, I can't help but think he'll turn me down. Lately it seems like he can't even be in the same room with me for more than a few minutes. I don't really see him voluntarily spending three weeks alone with me."

"You may be right, but you'll drive yourself crazy over this until you man up and ask."

Dane noticed the time. Did he dare bother Professor Sofokleous at home? He could always wait until Monday, but with winter break only seven days away Magnus would probably appreciate the extra weekend to prepare for the trip down south. "Okay, I'll talk to him."

"Good luck."

"Thanks. I'll need it, both with Professor Sofokleous and with my mother. She has a thing about having us all home for Christmas."

"If she knows you like I do, she'll understand."

Dane snorted. "You don't know my mother. She's the dictator of the family."

"Then you just have to ask yourself what's more important, making her mad or easing yourself into Magnus' bed."

"No brainer there." Dane smiled to himself. "Thanks."

"No problem. I told you when I moved out I'd always be here for you."

"I know. I just wasn't sure you really meant it. Other people have said stuff like that and then wandered away never to be heard from again."

"I'm not those people," Bobby said.

"Yeah, I get that. I'll call you tomorrow, after I've had a chance to talk to Magnus." Dane's stomach churned at the idea of visiting Magnus at his home.

"I'll be here."

After Bobby hung up, Dane carried the grant application into the bedroom with him. He chaned his clothes before calling the number listed on the contact section of the application.

"Yes," Magnus answered, his voice gruffer than usual.

"Hi, Professor, it's Dane Jefferson. Sorry to bother you at home, but I have something I need to talk to you about. I was wondering if I could drop by your house for a few minutes."

"It's not really a good time."

This was precisely how he'd envisioned the phone call going. Magnus was trying to brush him off like he always did. "It's about the grant you applied for."

"Excuse me?"

Dane's heart skipped a beat when he heard a male voice in the background. Of course Magnus would be entertaining, it was Friday night. "If you have company, I can talk to you about the grant on Monday," he offered.

"My guest isn't important, but I fail to see how you could know anything about the grant request I submitted."

"Yes, well, that's one of the things I wanted to discuss with you." Dane could have told Magnus his connection to the Institute over the phone, but he knew it would be harder for his professor to turn him down in person.

"Give me thirty minutes to tie up loose ends," Magnus offered.

"Yes, sir," Dane said automatically.

A noise came from deep in Magnus' throat, but Dane couldn't tell what it meant. Was the man already irritated with him? "I really am sorry for bothering you when you're busy."

"The grant's what's important, nothing more."

"I guess I'll see you in thirty minutes then."

Magnus hung up without saying anything further. Dane shoved the phone into the pocket of his jeans, wondering if he'd ever be able to get a full conversation out of his professor.

* * * *

"Session over. Time for you to go," Magnus told the submissive he'd been training.

Darrell, the thirty-two-year-old who was new to the lifestyle, stared at Magnus' obvious erection. "Really?"

Magnus didn't bother to tell Darrell that the state of his cock had nothing to do with him. It was Dane's use of 'sir' that had caused an immediate reaction in Magnus' body. Although Magnus had asked his teaching assistant to stop calling him sir on several occasions, Dane still address him as such. Magnus seriously doubted Dane was into the lifestyle, so more than likely the younger man had been raised in a southern household.

When Darrell continued to stare up at him without getting out of bed, Magnus began to lose his temper. "Do I need to repeat myself, boy?"

With a dramatic sigh, Darrell swung his legs over the side of the bed and stood. Magnus received a measure of satisfaction by looking at Darrell's bright red ass. If he'd had the time, he would have given Darrell a few more welts to remind him that insubordination wasn't tolerated.

Instead, Magnus headed for the bathroom. "Let yourself out."

"Yes, sir," Darrell said, reaching for his suit pants.

It didn't surprise Magnus that Darrell's use of sir didn't stir him in the slightest. It had become harder and harder to find a sub he actually yearned to dominate. An image of Dane naked and bent over his desk came to mind as Magnus stepped into the shower. *Fuck.*

Magnus reached down and wrapped his hand around his cock. He couldn't even be in the same room with Dane for more than five minutes without the urge to order him to his knees.

Magnus released his cock. He hated that thoughts of Dane could make his control slip. It was the primary reason he'd given Dane the job as his teaching assistant. Playing around with college men at the club was one thing, but he had a strict rule about not fucking students he taught.

When he'd discovered Dane's intention to remain at the college to obtain his postgraduate degree, Magnus knew he had to put some walls into place. Although seeing Dane on a daily basis had become almost unbearable, in his mind Dane was off limits.

Magnus finished washing before turning off the water. He opened the glass door and was surprised to find Darrell standing in the doorway. The anger that had been building towards himself was unleashed on the accountant. "I told you to get out," he growled.

"I know, but we usually set another time before I leave," Darrell explained.

In that moment, Magnus was able to see that Darrell had just been a poor substitute for the man he really wanted. "I think this arrangement has run its course. I'm sure you won't have a problem finding someone else to take up your training."

"But...I thought we had something special."

Naked, Magnus took a step forward, towering over Darrell. "Your mistake. I told you up front I don't get emotionally involved. Yes or no?"

Darrell looked down at the tiled floor. "Sure, but..."

"Nope. Stop right there. I'm a man who means what he says." Magnus wasn't a completely heartless ass. "Sorry I let it go on between us as long as it did. I should've seen it sooner."

Darrell turned and walked out of the room, leaving Magnus to wonder why he bothered having sex at all. Although he enjoyed the physical act, the drama most men brought to the bedroom wasn't worth it.

No matter how hard he tried, he would never understand why someone would willingly weaken themselves by allowing their emotions to lead them around by the nose. As a boy, he'd witnessed his father push and order his mother around in the name of love, stupid woman. She should have shoved a knife in her husband's gut and rid herself of the burden. Instead, she'd taken her heartache out on Magnus. Ninety per cent of the time, Magnus' father would disappear for a few days after a big fight, leaving a bitter and angry wife behind.

Once Magnus was old enough to fend for himself it hadn't been nearly as bad, but memories of being so hungry he'd often resort to eating the dog's food continued to haunt him. By the time he was a teenager, he'd become an expert at living life without emotional entanglements.

After the front door slammed shut, signalling Darrell's departure, Magnus crossed the room to his dresser. He started to reach for a clean pair of jeans but stopped and opened his closet instead. Magnus selected a crisp, freshly starched white dress shirt and pair of olive green cotton pants and tossed them onto the bed. It was important to keep their professional relationship intact.

Magnus dressed quickly before running a brush through his drying hair. Curls had begun to form, signalling it was time for a cut. He much preferred the sleek black waves to the curls that reminded him of the boy in the mirror so long ago.

By the time the doorbell rang, Magnus had pulled himself together. He shut the door to the bedroom and took a quick glance around the living room. Thankfully, his sessions with Darrell hadn't included wining and dining him, so the room was still in pristine order.

With his small wire-rimmed reading glasses in place, Magnus opened the door. "Come in, Dane."

Dane entered the house, his battered leather messenger bag slung over his shoulder. "Thanks. Sorry for interrupting your evening."

Magnus pointed Dane towards the sofa as he took a seat in his large leather recliner. "I've already told you, you didn't interrupt anything important. Now, what is this about the grant application I submitted?"

Dane set his bag on the floor beside his foot and removed a thin red folder. He fingered the pages inside before clearing his throat. It was clear to Magnus that the man was nervous.

"My mother passed your application on to me. She usually deals with this sort of thing, but she recognised your name and thought it would be best for me to handle it," Dane began.

"I don't understand. Does your mother work for the Institute?"

"Yes and no. You see, James D Barrett was my fourth great-grandfather on my mother's side. Mother, along with my two uncles, is on the board of directors at the Institute."

Magnus stared at Dane. He'd known Dane came from a wealthy family, but he had no idea his teaching assistant was connected to the Barrett fortune. "I didn't realise that."

Dane set the folder on the coffee table. "I have a couple of questions about the application before I can approve it."

"Okay." Magnus scooted to the edge of the chair and rested his forearms on his knees.

"Well, my question is twofold, really. First, I'd like to know what you'd be looking for at Barrett House? Second, would it be possible for me to assist you in your research? I need the field hours, and, as you can imagine, this is something I have a vested interest in."

Magnus took off his glasses and rubbed his eyes before resettling them. It was a risk to tell Dane what he'd already discovered, but it might prove an even greater risk to work alongside Dane in the field. "Do my answers determine whether or not I receive the grant?"

Dane sat up straighter on the couch. "I really want to assist you on this, Professor, but I'm not so self-centred that I would turn the grant down because you don't want me there."

Magnus wondered what Dane would say if he knew how much he was wanted, but it was too dangerous. "I can answer part of the first question." Magnus stood and retrieved a box from his floor safe, carefully setting it on the table beside the red folder. He lifted the lid to reveal a ceremonial necklace. "I came across this last summer while visiting an elderly MOWA Choctaw woman in Alabama. She agreed to give it to me with the promise that it never be sold and will eventually be put on display for all to enjoy."

Dane leaned closer. Shaking his head as he examined the beadwork, it was obvious he'd studied enough Native American history to identify the problem. "Have you had this authenticated?"

Magnus knelt on the floor beside the coffee table. "The beads are over a hundred years old, but the secret of who strung them together remains a mystery."

Magnus never tired of studying the ceremonial necklace. Built in intricate rows of beadwork, four Native American nations were represented, something Magnus had never before heard of. He glanced up at Dane. "According to the woman, the piece had been handed down through her family for generations. Unfortunately, the story behind it was lost except for a few details."

"Which are?" Dane asked, making eye contact.

Magnus took a deep breath. "The necklace came from the sole survivor of a tribe living on the Barrett plantation."

"Do you believe her?"

"I've got no reason not to. Forgive me, but it's always seemed strange to me that your family would fund a Native American history institute when, as far as my research goes, you're family's about as white as they come."

"Mother believes it's because James Barrett befriended a local tribe and was furious when the government drove them out of Louisiana. According to her, James promised them a piece of their history would always remain in the bayou."

Magnus nodded. "I believe they left more that has yet to be discovered."

Dane looked at the necklace again. "Okay, I agree it's something that should be explored further. I'll see that the grant is approved." Dane picked up the folder and put it away. "Umm...about the other thing..."

"I'll think about it," Magnus answered, cutting Dane off before he could continue.

Dane stood and shouldered his bag. "There are areas of the plantation that aren't open to anyone but family members." He met Magnus' gaze. "It would be in your best interest to have me along."

Magnus narrowed his eyes. Although Dane was clearly challenging him, Magnus found it enlightening. Perhaps Dane wasn't the pushover Magnus had always assumed him to be. "Like I told you, I'll think about it."

"Okay. My uncle Fallon lives in Morgan City. I'll call him, and have him prepare the Barrett House for your arrival. The Institute will be closed to the public from December 18th to January 9th, but there will still be maintenance workers there on and off during that period."

Magnus walked Dane to the door. "Thanks for the grant."

Dane stepped outside into the bitter cold evening. "I envy you," he mumbled. "Sure would be nice to get a break from this weather for a few weeks."

"Don't try so hard, kid," Magnus growled. "I'll give you my answer on Monday." Magnus watched Dane until he made it to his sleek Mercedes sports car. The damn thing probably cost more than Magnus' house.

Magnus shut the door and locked it before grabbing a beer out of the refrigerator. It was going to be a long weekend.

Chapter Two

Magnus did his best to avoid Dane on Monday morning, but by afternoon he knew his time was growing short. He'd racked his brain all weekend, trying to come up with a good, work-related excuse not to take Dane with him to Louisiana.

Magnus prided himself on keeping his personal life at home. Dane's request was business, not personal, and Magnus needed to conduct himself accordingly. If he left his personal desires for Dane out of the decision, he knew it made sense to take Dane. Not only would another pair of eyes help in the search, but also Dane's familiarity with the island on which the plantation sat could prove invaluable.

When the knock on the door came, Magnus took a deep breath. "Come in."

Dane, looking like a complete nerd in his khaki pants and argyle sweater vest, entered the office. He stood just inside the door and adjusted his glasses. "Sir, did you have time to consider who you'll take with you on Friday?"

Once again, Dane's use of 'sir' had an immediate effect on Magnus' body. "I'm getting damn tired of telling you to stop calling me that."

"Sorry." Dane's head lowered.

Fuck! Magnus took the opportunity to reach under his desk and readjust his cock to a more comfortable position. As he continued to stare at Dane, one thing became perfectly clear. He would never be able to work in the field with Dane and keep his hands to himself. Maybe it would be better to work Dane out of his system while they were away, rather than spend the next two years driving himself crazy. If something did happen between them in Louisiana, Magnus would just have to make it clear it would be over by the time winter break ended.

The more Magnus thought about it, the more he liked the idea of spending his days researching the Barrett plantation and his nights fucking Dane. "I'll leave right after I turn in final grades on Friday. Be ready to go or you'll stay here."

Dane's expression brightened. "You mean it? Really?"

Magnus leaned his forearms on the desk. "Let's get something straight. I never say anything I don't mean. Now, you should get going on those tests that need to be graded."

"Yes, sir…" Dane shook his head. "Sorry, Professor."

Dane turned and opened the office door. Unfortunately, he misjudged and kicked the edge of the door, which bounced back and nearly hit him in the face.

Magnus quickly covered a chuckle and looked down at the paperwork in front of him as if he hadn't seen the clumsy move. He glanced up again once he heard the door shut. Dane was too damn cute for his own good. Magnus hoped he could keep his hands off his newest field assistant long enough to get some work done.

* * * *

Dane spent the next four days grading papers, taking two final exams and packing. As he stood over his open suitcase, he tried to imagine what kind of clothes he'd need for the weeks ahead.

He'd worked on field locations before, but never with Professor Sofokleous. Of course, the other consideration was the terrain in which they'd be working. The Barrett plantation was an island, often referred to as a hummock, surrounded by a series of slow-moving rivers and streams.

As far as Dane knew, the island had only flooded three times since Barrett House was built. Although most people called it a plantation, the Barrett property never really produced enough rice to warrant the name. Dane believed it was the palatial yellow house on stilts more than anything that had given the island its name.

Going back to the clothes he'd selected, Dane took out all but one pair of khaki pants and replaced them with jeans. Not the designer jeans his mom insisted on buying him, but good old-fashioned Levis. There was something about the feel and fit of broken-in Levis that the expensive jeans lacked.

He tossed in some V-neck T-shirts and a few long-sleeved shirts — in case the weather turned cool — and a heavy red sweatshirt. Whether the professor would approve of his attire, Dane had no way of knowing, but he wasn't about to call him and ask what he was wearing. He may have discussed his clothes with

Bobby on occasion, but Bobby didn't give a shit that Dane was neurotic at times.

"What do you think, Ares?" he asked the German Shepherd, sleeping peacefully beside the bed.

Dane continued to stare at the suitcase, second guessing himself once again. "Oh, hell." He picked up the phone and called his best friend.

"Helloooo," Bobby answered in a sing-song voice.

"You're in a good mood." Dane collapsed on the bed beside his suitcase.

"Why shouldn't I be? We're picking Mom up at the airport in a few hours and Chet asked me to go without underwear for the drive. You know what that means?"

Dane laughed. "Yeah, the two of you will be lucky to make it to the airport in one piece."

"Sure, it's a risk, but you gotta admit, there's nothing better than getting a handjob in the car. Well, unless it's a blowjob, but Chet draws the line at a handjob, so I'll take what I can get."

Dane couldn't admit to anything. He'd never had a boyfriend that he'd ridden around with, so he wouldn't have a clue if a handjob in the car was as exciting as Bobby made it out to be. Although Dane was indeed a fan of giving blowjobs, he couldn't imagine doing it while someone was trying to drive. It all sounded incredibly dangerous and stupid. "I'll take your word for it," he finally answered.

Bobby laughed. "Oh, you wait, someday soon that big Greek of yours will be driving you somewhere and his cock'll be right there and you won't be able to stop yourself."

"Have you even met Professor Sofokleous? I seriously doubt he's the kind of guy who gets off on sex in the car." Dane crossed his legs and squeezed them together. He refused to touch his hardening cock while on the phone with Bobby.

The question set Bobby off into another round of laughter. "Dude, how can you claim to be in love with Magnus if you know nothing about him? I've got this kid in my marketing class who told me Magnus was the best fuck in the whole town. Apparently he really gets off on spanking, so I'd watch my ass if I were you."

Dane was completely offended that other students were discussing the Professor's personal life. "The guy's a liar. He's probably never even met Professor Sofokleous."

Bobby's laughter faded away immediately. "Dane? He was talking about D/s, ya know, Dominance and submission. Evidently, Magnus is into that shit. I'm sorry, I thought you knew."

Although Dane had been sheltered from anything left of centre for most of his life, he knew there were people out there who got off on role-playing and stuff like that. He wondered how far into it the Professor was. Dane rolled his eyes. He knew if he ever hoped to get into Magnus' bed, he needed to think of him as something other than his professor. *He has a name, use it*, he told himself.

The idea that *Magnus* would somehow try to control him didn't sit well with Dane. It had taken him years to break out from under his family's thumb and he wasn't about to let someone else dictate his life for him.

"You there?" Bobby asked.

"Yeah, I'm here." Dane decided to change the subject. "I'm packing and I wanted your opinion on jeans and T-shirts. You think they're enough or should I pack nicer stuff, too?"

"When in doubt, toss in a pair of slacks and maybe a jacket. You can wear them with a T-shirt if you have to. At least it would be good enough to get you into most places should the need arise. What's Professor Sofokleous taking?"

"I don't know. I'm afraid to call and ask him," Dane admitted.

"But if you need something special wouldn't it be better to find out now rather than later?"

"Yeah." Dane tossed it around in his head for a few moments. "Okay, I'll give him a call."

"Good, boy. You still coming over tomorrow night for popcorn and movies? My mom's anxious to meet you."

"I'll be there. I've got to bring Ares by anyway. Thanks for watching him for me while I'm gone."

"I've been looking forward to it. See you around six."

Dane hung up and immediately called Magnus.

"Yes, Dane," Magnus answered.

"How'd you know it was me?"

"Because your name popped up on caller ID. What can I do for you?"

"Oh, jeez, why didn't I think of that?" Dane slapped his palm against his forehead. "Umm, okay, I was wondering about clothes and what you're wearing?"

"At the moment? Nothing," Magnus said, a chuckle in his voice.

Dane felt his face heat. Could this be any more awkward? "No, I mean, I'm packing and I'm not sure if jeans and T-shirts are okay."

"That's what I'm packing," Magnus said.

"Good. I know I'm being a pest, I'm just really excited. I promise I won't bother you again." *Please don't be mad at me*, Dane silently prayed.

"To be perfectly honest, I was just sitting here wondering if I should pack something nice in case I meet your uncle," Magnus confessed.

Although Fallon was out and proud, Dane had never considered the possibility that Magnus might be interested. "I think Uncle Fallon will be in Austin with the rest of the family for the holidays."

Magnus was quiet for several seconds. "All right, then I guess it'll just be the two of us. I suppose that means work clothes are all we need."

Why did it sound like Magnus was sorry Fallon wouldn't be around? Dane didn't want to make an issue of it, so he tucked it away to worry about later. "Jeans it is. Well, I'll let you get back to...whatever it was you were doing."

"Dane?"

Dane took a deep breath. "Yeah?"

"We'll be working closely for the next three weeks and it would help if you could learn to relax."

Relax? How in the world would Dane be able to relax when his body remained on high alert around Magnus. He brushed the front of his sweats with the palm of his hand. Yep, despite feeling awkward and inferior during his conversation with Magnus, his body had still reacted predictably.

"Did you hear me?" Magnus prompted, obviously expecting an answer.

"I'll try."

"I have to post grades tomorrow, but I should be ready to leave in plenty of time to make our two o'clock flight. We'll leave straight from my office, so be there by noon," Magnus said before hanging up.

Dane glanced at the clock after the call ended. He had exactly fifteen hours to learn everything he could about the D/s lifestyle. Despite what he'd told Bobby,

Dane knew very little about it except what he'd seen in the occasional porno, but he had heard the term 'sir' used in them. He wasn't sure if he'd like what he'd find, but at least he'd go into it with his eyes wide open.

Dane tossed the phone onto the bed. He headed downstairs to his office. Packing could wait; his education couldn't.

* * * *

Dane sat outside Magnus' office in a daze. He'd managed to finish packing, he hoped. His head was full of the information he'd read online. Although he'd always thought of himself as a bottom, he doubted he could reach sexual fulfilment by allowing someone else to dominate him.

Sure, there were some aspects of the lifestyle that turned him on, but the rest made him extremely uneasy. He'd managed to reach adulthood without ever being subjected to corporal punishment. The whole idea of voluntarily allowing someone to spank him was absurd. He kept telling himself it was one aspect of Magnus' lifestyle, but it was completely off limits as far as Dane was concerned.

It had been only hours earlier that Dane's dreams had shattered. How many years had he fantasised about what it would feel like to be fucked by the great Magnus Sofokleous? To find out the two of them wouldn't be compatible in the bedroom broke Dane's heart. He'd even considered cancelling his involvement in the professor's research project. It was his love for anthropology and the Barrett family that had convinced him to put aside his personal feelings for Magnus and find out the truth about Barrett House.

Dane jumped in his seat when the door beside him opened. Magnus stood over him dressed in faded jeans and a tight black T-shirt. *Oh, hell.* Despite Dane's earlier decision, he felt his resolve beginning to slip.

"Ready?" Magnus asked.

Dane pushed his glasses up and got to his feet. *No!* He wanted to scream. "Ready."

"I've made arrangements for Professor Demakis to take us to the airport. He should be downstairs waiting for us." Magnus retrieved his suitcases from the office before closing and locking the door. "Where're your things?"

Dane dug a set of keys out of his pocket. "I'm sorry. I left them in the car. I was going to offer to drive us to the airport."

Magnus chuckled. "You really think I'd be able to fit in that little car of yours?"

Dane's chin dropped to his chest and he shook his head. "I'm sorry. I wasn't thinking."

Magnus reached out and ruffled Dane's hair. "Don't apologise. It was nice of you to offer. I shouldn't have laughed."

The apology warmed Dane more than he cared to admit. "I'll just run and get my suitcases and meet you out front."

"No need. I'm sure Alec won't mind driving around to the student parking lot." Magnus hoisted two large, olive-green duffle bags, one on each shoulder, and headed down the hall.

Dane had to jog to catch up to his mentor. He followed Magnus downstairs to the front of the building where Alec and Max were waiting. Except for seeing them at a barbecue before school had started, Dane didn't really know either of the men.

"Do you mind driving around to the student lot to get Dane's luggage?" Magnus asked, tossing his bags into the back of the dual-cab pickup.

"Not at all," Alec answered.

Magnus opened the door and gestured for Dane to get in. Dane climbed into the truck and scooted across the bench seat.

"I really appreciate this," Dane told Alec.

Alec studied Dane in the rearview mirror for a moment before answering. "No problem."

Dane watched as Alec's gaze swung to Magnus. "You sure about this?" Alec asked Magnus.

"Just drive," Magnus fired back.

Dane looked at Magnus. He wasn't sure what was going on between the two friends, but, whatever it was, Magnus seemed suddenly to be on edge. Magnus turned his head to stare out of the side window.

"So, I hear you're rich," Max said, surprising Dane.

"Umm…" Dane wasn't sure how to answer.

"Max," Alec growled his partner's name.

"Sorry." Max glanced over his shoulder. "Sometimes I talk without thinking it through first."

"That's okay. I do the same thing." Dane glanced at Magnus who was still staring out of the window. "I learned to manage investments when I was still in high school. Although my family is rather wealthy, my portfolio doesn't compare to theirs. It all started in elementary school right after my Aunt Amelia passed away. She…"

Dane stopped himself. Not only was the truck stopped beside his Mercedes SLK, but all eyes were on him. *Fuck.* He opened the door and slid out of the truck. Max hadn't asked him for a breakdown of his financial situation.

Dane opened the trunk and reached for his leather suitcases. He used to blame his parents for his awkwardness around other kids, but somewhere between his freshman and sophomore year of college he'd realised he simply wasn't interesting enough to fit in with most people. Now, not only would Magnus realise it, but so would Max and Alec.

"You need help?" Magnus asked, reaching for Dane's luggage.

Dane shook his head. "Thanks, but I can get them." He hoisted both suitcases out of the trunk. "I'm sorry if I embarrassed you in front of your friends."

Magnus' jaw muscle twitched. "You didn't. Let's just get going or we'll miss our flight."

"Yes, sir." Dane allowed Magnus to take one of the suitcases. He silently cursed himself for using the formal address, but it had been drilled into him as a child.

Magnus paused in the process of stowing the luggage. He stared down at Dane like a hungry man looking at a juicy steak.

Dane's body reacted predictably. Damn his traitorous cock.

Alec honked the horn, breaking the spell between them.

Magnus finished with Dane's suitcases before opening the door. "After you."

Like he had earlier, Dane climbed in and scooted over, putting himself on the opposite side of the truck. He was glad he didn't have Alec's eyes on him all the time; let Magnus deal with the concerned looks for a change.

* * * *

With his eyes closed, Magnus grabbed the arm of the seat as the plane took off. He'd always hated flying. Unfortunately, in this case it was unavoidable.

Dane leaned against Magnus' side and spoke into his ear. "You okay?"

Magnus opened his eyes and sat up. "I'm fine." He cursed himself for showing weakness in front of Dane. "Just tired."

"You can lean against me if you want to sleep," Dane offered.

Magnus shook his head. "I should be working. How long will it take to get to Barrett House after we land and pick up the rental car?"

"Depends. If Uncle Fallon arranged a boat, like he said he would, it'll take about twenty or thirty minutes to get to the dock, another half hour to the island." Dane grabbed Magnus' wrist and held it up so he could see the time. "We should be there by six, I'd say."

The simple contact took Magnus' mind off the flight and put it squarely on Dane. It would be too dark to start work that night. Maybe the two of them could find something equally as pleasurable to do inside. The thought surprised him. In the past, his work had always come first. Sex hadn't remotely compared to the thrill of the hunt.

With Dane's touch lingering, Magnus turned his hand over to brush against Dane's. "We'll have to start tomorrow then. Perhaps tonight we can use the time to get to know each other better."

Dane started to speak, but stopped to clear his throat before proceeding. "What did you have in mind?"

Magnus wondered if it was too early to lay his cards on the table. If Dane wasn't interested in a short-term affair, it would definitely make the next three weeks awkward, but if Dane said yes there was no reason to waste time dancing around each other.

"I don't get involved with my students," Magnus said, low enough for only Dane to hear.

"I know that," Dane mumbled.

Magnus moved his hand to rest on Dane's thigh. "For the next three weeks, I'm a fellow anthropologist, not a professor. If you're interested...?" Magnus left the sentence unfinished. He watched Dane's Adam's apple bob up and down several times.

"I'm not sure we'd be a good fit for each other," Dane eventually said.

"What's that supposed to mean?"

Dane took a deep breath, casting his eyes downward. "Your lifestyle. I don't think it's something I could handle. My parents never believed in punishing me. I don't think I could handle a lover doing it just to get off."

"Punishing you? Is that what you think I want to do to you?" The insinuation that he couldn't fuck without hurting someone to get off was a slap in the face.

"I looked it up on the Internet," Dane began.

Magnus held up a hand to stop Dane. "That's your first mistake. If you wanted to know what *gets me off*, you should have asked me."

"And would you have answered?"

"Probably not," Magnus conceded. "But I'll answer now if you care to ask."

Dane glanced around at the small plane full of passengers. "Later, if it's okay with you?"

"Fine." Magnus settled his hands back on the armrests. He tried to picture Dane laid out over his lap as he used a paddle to warm his trim little ass. The image started to make Magnus hard until the Dane in his dream cried out in pain. Magnus quickly pushed the thought aside along with the way it made him feel.

Dane rested his hand on top of Magnus'. "I've wanted to be with you for a long time. The thought just scares me, I guess. Please don't be angry."

Magnus looked down into Dane's eyes. "Are you a virgin?"

Dane shook his head. "I've dated, but I'm not a slut or anything."

Magnus threaded his fingers through Dane's. It was a different feeling for him. He came close to releasing Dane's hand and calling the whole thing off. "We'll talk later."

* * * *

Magnus parked the rental car in the small parking lot. "Who's that?"

Dane groaned when he glanced towards the dock. *Shit.* What was Fallon doing here? "My uncle."

"I thought you said he wouldn't be here." Magnus pocketed the keys and popped the trunk before climbing out of the car.

By the time Dane got out, Magnus was already walking towards the dock with both of his bags and one of Dane's suitcases. Dane grabbed the last suitcase and shut the trunk. It looked like Magnus and Fallon were already getting acquainted.

Dane's hopes plummeted. Fallon was gorgeous. No way would Magnus look twice at Dane with Fallon around. He started towards the small flat-bottomed boat.

"Monkey!" Fallon called out. He stepped on to the dock to wrap his arms around Dane in greeting.

Dane dropped his suitcase and hugged his uncle. "I thought you were going home."

"I am, but I thought I'd stay long enough to see you and get the two of you settled first." Fallon stepped back and picked up Dane's bag. "You look good."

"Thanks." The moment Dane stepped into the boat he noticed the smirk on Magnus' handsome face. "What?"

"Monkey?" Magnus questioned.

Dane shrugged. "I climbed trees a lot when I was a kid." He sat on one of the three benches facing towards the front of the boat. He couldn't believe Fallon had called him by the childhood name in front of Magnus.

"Why don't you turn around so I can actually see your face while we talk?" Fallon said, starting the trolling motor on the small flat-bottomed boat.

"That's okay, I like to see where I'm going," Dane answered over his shoulder.

"Fine. If you won't talk to me now, I'll just have to stay for dinner and catch up," Fallon threatened.

With a dramatic sigh, Dane turned around to face his uncle. Unfortunately, the new position also put his knees within touching distance of Magnus'. "So, how's business?" he asked Fallon.

"Good. As a matter of fact, I've been talking to Tony Bianchi about a joint venture."

Dane shook his head. Fallon had crushed on Tony since they'd gone to college together. It had been Fallon's connection to Tony that had secured Dane's purchase of Tony's mansion. "Don't forget Tony has a partner now."

"I know that." Fallon grinned. "At least if he agrees to the deal I'll be in place when the two of them break up."

Dane decided to use the moment to warn Magnus off Fallon. "You'll have to excuse my uncle. He's under the mistaken impression that Daniel Willis isn't right for Tony."

"He's not," Fallon argued. "How could someone as brilliant as Tony be content living with a potter? It's ridiculous."

Dane glanced at Magnus. He knew Magnus was friends with Professor Willis and wondered if he would challenge a man as powerful as Fallon.

Right on time, Magnus took his eyes off the passing landscape and turned his attention to Fallon. "Tony's an incredibly imaginative and intelligent man. I think he and Daniel are perfectly suited for each other. I know they're very happy, so you may be waiting a long time if you're holding out for Tony."

Dane was impressed by the way Magnus managed to stick up for his friend while keeping the statement light enough not to offend. Regardless, Dane decided to soothe the pain he detected in his uncle's eyes. "You'll find someone younger and hotter than Tony."

Fallon blinked several times before smiling. "Sure I will. I find them all the time. Problem is, after a few weeks I find out they're only really interested in my money. I wouldn't have that worry with Tony."

"Maybe things would be different if you actually got to know them first," Dane reminded his uncle.

"I get to know them." Fallon winked. "Very well, in fact."

Without thought, Dane knocked knees with Magnus to get his attention. "Would you please tell my uncle there's more to getting to know a person than shoving a dick up their ass."

Magnus narrowed his eyes. "I've never heard you talk like that."

Dane's jaw dropped. Why did he feel like he'd just been scolded? Whatever the reason, Dane didn't like it. "I'm trying to make a point. It would be nice if you backed me up on this."

"Why? I have absolutely no say on where your uncle sticks his cock. And neither do you." Magnus trapped Dane's knees between his.

"Thank you, Magnus," Fallon said.

Dane stared into Magnus' big brown eyes. Had Magnus scolded him because he was jealous of Fallon's feelings for Tony? The two of them continued to watch each other for several moments before Magnus gave Dane a slight shake of his head. Dane wondered if his jealousy had been so transparent. He returned the gesture with a half-smile before breaking eye contact. "We're not in for any bad weather while we're here, are we?" he asked Fallon.

"Nope, not as far as I know." Fallon steered the boat down the winding waterway toward Barrett House.

By the time they reached the small island plantation, Dane couldn't get off the boat fast enough. He jumped to the dock and held his hand out for his suitcases. "Can you pass me those, Uncle Fallon?"

"I've got 'em," Magnus said.

"Thanks, but I can carry them," Dane countered.

Magnus set Dane's luggage on the dock beside him. "Suit yourself."

Dane grabbed the suitcases and started up the boardwalk to the crushed shell walkway that would eventually lead him to the house. He glanced over his shoulder only to find Fallon and Magnus deep in conversation about something. With a resigned sigh, Dane continued on his way. He couldn't keep the two men apart if they were determined to start something, so why try.

Magnus watched Dane take off up the boardwalk without even telling his uncle goodbye. "I think he's tired after the flight," he told Fallon.

Fallon stepped up on the dock to stand in front of Magnus. "Not sure what you have planned for my nephew, but if you think you can come down here and screw him over you've got another think coming. Do I make myself clear?"

Magnus wasn't intimidated easily. "Dane's a grown man. Best you leave him to make his own decisions."

He shouldered his duffle bags and turned to follow Dane. A hand on his arm brought him up short. Although Fallon Barrett matched Magnus in size, the rich playboy didn't have half Magnus' survival skills. "I would suggest you take your hand off me while you're still able to drive yourself back to the mainland."

"I could cancel the grant and send you back where you came from," Fallon threatened.

"And are you going to be the one to break it to Dane?"

Fallon narrowed his eyes before releasing Magnus. "I love that little Monkey. He's a good boy who deserves better than you."

"I won't argue with you there." Magnus walked away with his heart in his throat. It wasn't often he allowed someone to make him feel as worthless as he had when he was a child, but Fallon was only trying to protect someone he loved. Magnus could and did respect that.

Chapter Three

Dane struggled up the wide staircase with his luggage, but he wasn't about to admit it to Magnus. "The guest quarters are on the third floor," he explained as he walked down the second-floor hall to a smaller staircase. "It used to be the servants' floor."

Magnus followed closely. "Didn't we just pass about eight other bedrooms?"

"Yeah, but those are part of the tour. Guests always stay up here. You'll like it. A lot more luxurious than the ones on the second level." Dane reached the top of the stairs and walked down the long hallway. "When I come with my parents they always stick me in the smaller room, so I'll take the bigger one this time. You can sleep in Fallon's." It was probably a childish thing to say, but Dane said it anyway.

Dane was surprised when Magnus followed him into the bedroom. He turned and looked up at the handsome man. "Fallon's room is across the hall."

Magnus dropped his bags and wrapped an arm around Dane's waist, pulling him close. "I don't care where Fallon's room is. I'd much rather stay in here with you."

As Magnus lowered his head, Dane knew it was a decisive moment. Did he push his professor away out of fear or sink into the arms of the man he'd worshipped for years?

Magnus slowly lowered his head. "Trust me," he whispered a moment before he pressed his lips against Dane's.

Dane counted to three before dropping his luggage. He wrapped his arms around Magnus' neck as he opened his mouth to his questing tongue. *Oh. My. God.* The taste and feel of Magnus was so much more than Dane had ever imagined.

Magnus took control of the kiss, sharing his skills with an impressed Dane. When Dane felt Magnus' strong hands grab and squeeze his ass, he couldn't help but moan. He whimpered when he felt his feet leave the floor. As Dane's cock was pressed against Magnus' erection, he witnessed his first moment of being mastered. The kiss had only just begun and already he'd given his control to Magnus. Would he regret it? He still didn't believe in allowing another person to strike him in any fashion. Dane could think of more enjoyable ways for Magnus to use his hands.

Magnus withdrew his tongue and slowly lowered Dane to his feet. "We should talk."

"Now?" Dane asked. He pressed his erection against Magnus' thigh.

Magnus grasped Dane by the shoulders and took a step back, putting space between them. "I'm serious. Your uncle warned me not to hurt you, so that's what I'm trying to avoid." He walked over to the bed and sat on the edge of the mattress.

"Pay no attention to Fallon. He's probably just jealous." Dane sat next to Magnus and crossed his legs under him.

Magnus leaned over and brushed his lips across Dane's. "He loves you. Even I can't fault him for being protective. You don't exactly strike me as a worldly kind of guy. Actually, that's what worries me. Never, in all the years I've taught, have I slept with one of my students."

"Are you afraid I'll use our relationship to get a better grade or something?" Dane began. He had his own reservations about getting involved with Magnus, but none of them were professional. "Because I can assure you I would never do something like that."

Magnus shook his head. "I don't know if I'm willing to take that chance. I'd like the two of us to enjoy our time while we're here, but I need to warn you of something. I don't get emotionally involved with my partners."

"Why?" Dane couldn't imagine opening himself to Magnus only to be rebuffed emotionally.

"Emotion is a weakness I don't allow myself." Before Dane could speak, Magnus held up a finger. "And, I'm not sure what *lifestyle* you think I'm involved in, but I assure you no harm will come to you in my bed."

Dane decided to put aside his questions regarding Magnus' fear of emotions and focus on the immediate problem at hand. "So, you're not going to make me sit at your feet and call you sir?"

Magnus chuckled. "No, I won't make you sit at my feet, but feel free to call me sir while we're here."

"I was right. You do like it when I call you that."

"Of course I like it. It's a show of respect. What man wouldn't want a verbal reminder of where he stands with a lover?"

"You mean you're not into the whole D/s stuff? But you hang out at that club."

Magnus stood and walked to the window. "Have you ever been in Lucky's?"

"Of course not. I know what goes on there."

"Then you know it's nothing but a place to hook up for uncomplicated sex." Magnus rested his palms on either side of the window, refusing to look at Dane. "Like-minded men who let me set the rules when we're together. I need that."

Dane climbed off the bed. "Why do you need that?" He didn't expect Magnus to answer, but he had to ask.

Magnus pushed away from the window and turned to stare down at Dane. "Because they let me fuck them without asking questions," he grumbled. "Maybe you should try it."

Dane held his hands up in surrender. "Fine, but we're not at the club and I'm definitely not one of your boys you can order around." He picked up his luggage and turned towards the door. "I'll take Fallon's room."

* * * *

Magnus found Dane on the expansive porch that surrounded the house. He'd managed to wait over an hour before going in search of the little pain in the ass. "Mind if I join you?"

Dane continued to stare out over the lush grounds. "Suit yourself."

Magnus took a deep, calming breath as he eased into one of the rattan rocking chairs. He wasn't used to explaining himself and resented the present urge to do so. Why was he breaking all his longstanding rules for the man beside him? "I survived my childhood by erecting walls. I need them."

"What happened when you were a child?" Dane asked, finally looking at Magnus.

Magnus shook his head. He wasn't ready or willing to let Dane into that portion of his life. "Let's just say my childhood was nothing like yours."

"So where does that leave us?"

"That depends. Will you be satisfied with the next three weeks? Because that's all I have to offer."

"I'm sorry." Dane stood. "It's not in me to settle for less than I deserve. When you can drop the bullshit, let me know."

A sense of inferiority began to creep its way inside Magnus. "No!" he shouted, exploding out of his chair. "You will not talk to me that way." He pushed Dane against the side of the house, trapping him with his body.

Magnus stared down into Dane's wide, frightened eyes. He hadn't even begun to let Dane see the real man he kept hidden and already Dane was afraid of him.

"I thought you said you'd never hurt me," Dane said.

Magnus closed his eyes and rested his cheek against the side of Dane's head. He felt like his insides were twisting into an unbearable knot of need. What surprised him was the source. The need to comfort Dane, to hold him, was more than Magnus could deny. "I won't," he promised. He knew of only one way to keep his word. After kissing the side of Dane's head, Magnus stepped back. "You were right. You deserve better."

Magnus took the porch steps two at a time until he reached the spongy green grass. Although the sun had already set, the grounds were illuminated by high-tech landscape lighting, allowing Magnus a safe escape.

Travelling along the narrow asphalt path, he eventually found a stone bench. "What's happening to me," he whispered to the thick night air. It was obvious his control was starting to slip where Dane was concerned. Magnus studied the surrounding area. He might be better off remembering why he had applied for the grant in the first place.

* * * *

After a fitful few hours of trying to sleep, Dane decided to spend the night in the library. The room had always brought him peace. Maybe it was the soft furniture or the smell of old leather books; whatever it was it felt like home to Dane.

He stretched out on the dark red leather sofa and stared at the wall of books. There was another building on the island that housed the research material and artefacts collected by the Institute, but the house had remained intact. The occasional book was borrowed from James Barrett's personal library, but for the most part the collection was just as James had left it.

Dane wondered if there was anything on the shelves that would tell him about the necklace Magnus had been given. *Magnus.* Dane swore he'd never be able to forget the pain he'd detected in Magnus' dark brown eyes. Whatever had happened in Magnus' childhood had followed him into adulthood. It felt strange to see a crack in the professor's iron control, but Dane had no doubt he'd witnessed it when he'd been pressed against the house.

Unfortunately, Magnus had fled before Dane could verbalise the way it made him truly feel. He should have been afraid. Magnus was almost twice his size, yet all Dane had felt was excitement at the prospect of being taken to bed by the handsome professor. Too bad he'd acted like a frightened child instead of the man he wanted Magnus to see him as.

This is my chance. If I let the next three weeks slip through my fingers, I'll always wonder what could have been. Dane got to his feet and retied his bathrobe. He made his way up the staircase and into Magnus' room.

Dane stood over Magnus' sleeping form. Bared to the waist, Magnus' body was perfection hidden under a blanket of short black hair. Unable to resist, Dane reached down and trailed his fingers through the soft curls.

Magnus stirred and opened his eyes. "What're you doing in here, Dane?"

Dane let his robe fall to the floor, exposing himself to Magnus. "I couldn't sleep," he said, turning on the small bedside lamp. Dane climbed onto the bed and straddled Magnus' body, seating himself on his groin. "I don't need to understand your past to know I want you."

Magnus settled his hands on Dane's hips, his thumbs brushing his pubic hair. "I thought I scared you."

"The only thing that scared me was how much I wanted you to tear off my clothes and fuck me right there against the house." Dane should've been mortified that he'd just admitted that but, instead, the hardening cock under his ass empowered him. He decided to push Magnus further. "Promise that sometime within the next three weeks you'll fuck me like you wanted to earlier."

Magnus' hand moved to stroke Dane's cock. "You sure you can handle that? I'm not known for my gentle nature when it comes to fucking."

Dane's teeth scraped his bottom lip as he eased down to lie on top of Magnus. He pushed the blankets off Magnus with his feet. A sigh escaped Dane's lips when he felt the full length of Magnus' impressive erection against him. "I think I've died and gone to heaven," he mumbled.

Magnus wrapped his arms around Dane and rolled them both until he was on top. Staring down at Dane, Magnus began to roll his hips, grinding his cock against him. He lowered his mouth over Dane's and thrust his tongue inside.

As the kiss deepened, Dane slid his legs around Magnus' waist. With a grunt of satisfaction, Magnus grabbed Dane's ass. He broke the kiss and whispered, "You sure about this?" against Dane's lips.

Dane tilted his head further back, giving Magnus access to his throat. "I'm sure."

Magnus' mouth latched on to the soft skin of Dane's neck. *Oh my God!* Dane had never felt anything like it. *I'm getting my first hickey,* he wanted to scream.

After several moments, Magnus released the suction on Dane's neck. "Perfect," he said, reaching for the nightstand. He rolled off Dane and opened the drawer, withdrawing a condom and small bottle of lube.

With his hair mussed, and his lips swollen from kissing, Magnus was even more drool-worthy than ever. Dane stretched his arms over his head, feeling rather giddy. "So, do you give hickeys to all the guys you sleep with?"

Magnus paused in the process of dripping lube onto his fingers. "I don't sleep with the men I fuck." He looked towards Dane's cock. "Although I plan to make an exception with you."

"So, that's really all this is to you? Just a fuck?" Dane had known going in that Magnus wasn't promising anything beyond their time in Louisiana, but it still hurt to hear.

Magnus settled beside Dane and propped his head on his hand. "If you need something more, then I'm not the right man for you."

There was something in Magnus' expression that didn't look right. "Are you trying to convince me or yourself?" Dane asked.

Magnus narrowed his eyes. "You're the one who came in, begging to be fucked. If you've changed your mind, just say so."

"No." Dane sobered. "I haven't."

"Good, then no more talking." Magnus circled Dane's asshole with a slicked finger.

Lying spread-eagled on the bed, Dane suddenly felt like Magnus was readying him for a prostate exam. He stared at the handsome face he'd grown to love and wondered why Magnus' touch felt so different than it had earlier in the day.

It wasn't until Dane studied Magnus' eyes that he suddenly knew the answer, but by then Magnus had worked a finger deep inside him. "Stop," Dane said.

"What?"

Dane slapped at Magnus' chest and tried to squirm away. "Just stop." He rolled off the bed and landed on his butt.

"What the hell is wrong with you?" Magnus asked.

Dane scrambled to reach his robe and put it on before standing. "I can't. I thought I could take whatever you had to give, but I like you too much to be just another number."

"You're not..." Magnus began.

"Don't," Dane cut him off. "Your touch is...clinical. It's like there's absolutely no emotion behind it at all. Hell, I might as well be any other man you picked up at the club." He rubbed his chest to soothe his breaking heart. "I just wish..." Dane shook his head and headed out of the room. "Forget it. I'll see you tomorrow."

* * * *

Showered and shaved, Magnus went in search of his assistant. The project was forefront in his mind after a night dissecting every moment of his time with Dane in bed. It hadn't been the first time he'd heard a similar description of his technique, but he'd never let it bother him before.

After a thorough search of the third floor, Magnus found Dane asleep on a massive bed on the second floor. He stepped further into the bedroom and opened the heavy green velvet drapes. Sun filtered into the room, shining light on the over-the-top decor.

The lump under the covers let out a groan, making Magnus smile for the first time in hours. "Rise and shine," he said.

The oil painting above the fireplace caught Magnus' attention. The imposing man in the foreground wasn't what caught his attention, however. It was the small solar cross etched into the stone behind James Barrett that captivated him.

"He was pretty handsome, huh?" Dane said, sitting up.

Magnus pointed towards the painting. "Where was this painted? Was it here on the island?"

Dane appeared beside Magnus, robe securely in place. "Are you talking about that rock?"

"Yeah." Magnus studied the rest of the painting. He spotted an eagle hidden within the tree branches. "There, do you see it?" He turned to look at Dane. "He wanted someone to know. Why else would he commission this painting?"

"Know what? I spent half my life searching this island for that spot. It's not here, Professor."

"It had to've been painted nearly a hundred and seventy-five years ago. Landscapes can change in that amount of time." Magnus pulled out his cell phone and took several pictures of the painting. "Get dressed."

"Give me five minutes to get dressed," Dane said on his way out of the room.

Magnus pocketed his phone and turned to study the rest of the room. He checked the other paintings, but nothing struck him as unusual. The heavily carved furniture was definitely period, but the bedding and drapes were obviously reproductions. He ran his fingers over the massive bedpost.

"Beautiful, isn't it?" Dane asked from the doorway.

"Very."

"It's all one piece. Evidently James Barrett had it built right here in this room." Dane walked over and started making the bed.

"Why'd you sleep in here?" Magnus asked.

Dane looked up at Magnus and smiled. "Growing up, I spent most of my summers here. My parents made that little room on the third floor mine, but it got really hot." He smoothed the bedspread in place. "I used to wait until I knew they were asleep and sneak down here." He pointed toward the French doors. "I would open those doors and the breeze from the balcony would blow in on the bed."

"Sounds nice," Magnus murmured. He couldn't imagine a childhood when the biggest problem of the day was where to sleep when the room got hot. No wonder he and Dane were so different. Magnus couldn't help but wonder how differently he would've turned out if only he'd had Dane's parents. He swallowed around the lump in his throat and turned toward the door. "Let's go."

* * * *

"Have you ever been here?" Dane asked as they neared the Institute building.

"Of course," Magnus answered.

Dane unlocked the door and preceded Magnus inside. Although much newer than the rest of the structures on the island, the Research Institute was designed and built to fit in with the existing buildings. "The maps are over here." Dane walked into the smaller room and turned on the overhead lights. "Of course, these are all copies. The originals are stored in the vault."

"These'll do. I just want to get a better feel for the island's layout."

Dane scanned the front of the document cabinets until he found the one he needed. He pulled out the wide drawer and removed a small stack of maps. He was acutely aware of how near Magnus was as he sat the maps on the table and began to go through them.

"Here it is." Dane took a step back to give Magnus some room.

Magnus put on his reading glasses and bent over the map. "There's a cemetery here?"

"Yeah, but there's not much there: two big mausoleums, a garden and a statue of James Barrett. It's one of the areas that's off limits to outsiders."

"Can I see it?" Magnus asked.

"Sure." Dane moved to Magnus' side and pointed towards a small strip of land across the water from the island. "That used to be part of the plantation, too, but it's a flood area. I know the Institute used to try and keep it up, but it became too costly according to my mother."

"Is there a way over there?"

"There's a boat, but, like I said, if there was ever something over there, it's probably been washed away by now." Looking at the map, Dane tried to figure out where Native Americans would've lived if they had truly been on the island. "What about this?" he asked, pointing towards an open field.

"My gut tells me no, but it won't hurt to check everything. I'd like to go through the cemetery first, though."

Dane groaned. The cemetery was his least favourite place on the island. It hadn't always been that way but once, while playing in one of the mausoleums, he'd managed to get himself locked inside the stone building when the iron gate had slammed shut. Surrounded by the burial chambers of his ancestors, the seven-year-old Dane had been trapped for almost six hours. It wasn't until he'd missed dinner that his family had begun to worry. After his rescue, his mother had made him promise never to go near the cemetery again.

It'll be different this time, Dane told himself as he led Magnus towards the cemetery. Not only was he years older, but he'd have Magnus with him. He left the crushed shell path and headed for a stand of trees. It was an area of the plantation that had reverted back to its natural state. According to his uncle, the family would rather the public didn't venture into the private area, so they'd done their best to make it unappealing.

"It's just beyond these trees," Dane said.

"No wonder I didn't know the cemetery existed."

"That's the idea." Dane produced a ring of keys from his pocket and unlocked the gate to the iron fence that surrounded the cemetery. By the expression on Magnus' face, Dane knew what his professor was thinking. "This is a Catholic cemetery, so, unless the Native Americans you think once lived here were Catholic, they wouldn't be here. Evidently James Barrett was very specific about that in his will."

Magnus stared up at the statue of James D Barrett. "He looks quite different than his portrait."

Dane nodded. "I think he commissioned it when he was a lot younger, right after his first wife died."

Magnus squatted beside the base and read the attached plaque. "The loss of one's soul forever changes the beauty of the landscape." With his arms still resting on his thighs, Magnus looked up at Dane. "He must have loved her very much."

Dane sat in the thick grass beside Magnus. "There's no written proof she even existed except for what's been chiselled on the outside of her burial chamber."

"Can I see it?" Magnus asked.

Dane stood and led the way to the mausoleum. "Oddly enough, James was encased right next to her, although his second wife, the one who bore his sons, isn't even in the same mausoleum." Dane pointed towards the smaller structure across the garden. "That's where Mary is along with their children, grandchildren and great-grandchildren."

Dane propped open the iron gate with a large stone he found beside the path and stepped back, allowing Magnus to enter first.

"So who's buried in here?" Magnus asked, stepping inside the cool interior.

"Just James and his first wife." Dane ran a hand over the words carved into the stone as he read the inscription. "My beloved. Your memory will forever be my purpose. November 19th, 1840." He glanced at Magnus. "We know James married Elizabeth ten years later but no written name for his first wife has ever been found."

"Your memory will forever be my purpose," Magnus reiterated. "What was his purpose?"

"To make as much money as possible?" Dane suggested. "In the years between 1840 and 1865, James almost tripled his net worth."

"How?"

"Nothing legal, that's for sure. The plantation wasn't large enough to amass that kind of money. The best guess is smuggling, but no one knows whether it was goods or slaves. Whichever it was, his sons evidently learned the trade because they continued in his footsteps in the 1920s, once prohibition was signed into law." Dane cleared his throat. "Of course, that's private information. As far as the rest of the world knows, the Bennett family came over from England with a fortune and learned to invest their money wisely."

Magnus chuckled. "Good to know the Bennett family isn't as squeaky clean as they claim to be."

Dane shrugged. "Every family has its skeletons."

Magnus' smirk disappeared. "Yeah, I suppose they do."

Chapter Four

Magnus sat at the dining table with his notes spread out in front of him. He kept going back to the inscription on James' first wife's burial chamber. *Your memory will forever be my purpose.*

Despite Dane's belief that making money was James' *purpose*, Magnus felt it went deeper. James had as much as admitted that he'd lost his soul when his first wife had died. Although it would explain why he'd gone into the smuggling trade, it didn't explain why there were no records of the woman he'd loved beyond a grave marker. *What were you hiding?*

"It's not much, but cooking really isn't my forte," Dane said, setting a pot of spaghetti on the table.

Magnus stared at the food. He hadn't asked Dane to prepare dinner, nor had he expected it, so why had Dane done it?

"I'm sorry, would you rather work?" Dane stood and reached for the pot.

"It's fine." Magnus reached out to stay Dane with a hand on his arm. "Sit."

Dane sank back into his chair. "What's going on?"

"Nothing." Magnus jerked his hand back. "I'm just not used to people cooking for me." He didn't go into detail, crying on someone's shoulder wasn't his thing. Instead, he filled his plate and sprinkled some Parmesan cheese over the top. "How did James get the money to buy the plantation in the first place?" he asked, hoping to distract Dane.

Dane swallowed a mouthful of food. "I don't know."

"What do you mean, you don't know? You have an entire research institute named after the guy. Surely you have to know everything there is to know about him."

Dane tilted his head to the side. "How far back can you trace your family tree? Do you know everything about your ancestors?" He tore off a hunk of bread. "Sorry. I think the family always had a little money, but I'm not sure where it came from."

Hell, Magnus didn't even know his grandparents, let alone anyone beyond that. "Fair enough."

"Why does it matter, anyway?"

Magnus wished he knew. None of it made sense, but he couldn't admit that to Dane. He'd never known the kind of love James had obviously had for his first wife. "If James was so devastated when his first wife died, how could he remarry?"

"He needed sons," Dane said as if the answer was obvious. "I told you, his grandson is responsible for setting up the Institute. I think James knew he had to do whatever it took to keep the plantation going."

Magnus continued to eat his dinner as he thought about what Dane had told him. It made sense that James would do what was necessary to continue his line. "This is good," he said around a mouthful of spaghetti.

"Thanks. It's my dad's recipe. Although he used to make it on Wednesday night. Saturday was pizza, but I don't really know how to make that."

"Your dad cooked?" Magnus asked.

"Sure, when it was his turn. My parents had a chef for a while, but Mom said it was putting a wedge between her family and she wouldn't have it." Dane grinned. "Mom usually gets what she wants, so we were all forced to cook twice a week, Saturdays being pizza night."

Once again, Magnus wondered what it would've been like to grow up in a normal household. From everything he'd heard, Magnus doubted Dane's dad had ever struck his wife, drunk or sober. "Sounds nice."

"Yeah, well, it might sound nice now, but, believe me, growing up I thought I was being mistreated," Dane said before chuckling.

"You don't know the first thing about being mistreated," Magnus snapped. He ate another bite of his dinner.

"You're right, I don't," Dane mumbled. "That was a thoughtless thing to say. I'm sorry."

Magnus finished his spaghetti without looking at Dane. The moment the last bite was in his mouth, he stood with his empty plate. "I'll do the dishes."

Magnus shook his head at the state of the kitchen. How could one man dirty so many dishes? It was spaghetti for cryin' out loud. He was in the process of filling the sink with hot soapy water when Dane carried his plate in.

"I'll dry," Dane offered.

Feeling especially vulnerable just then, Magnus knew it wasn't a good idea. "You cooked. I'll clean up." He reached for Dane's plate, but Dane held on until Magnus looked at him.

"I'll dry," Dane reiterated. "Doing trivial things with someone else heightens the experience."

When Dane pressed himself against Magnus' side, Magnus quickly reminded himself of their last sexual debacle. "What're you doing?"

"I don't know." Dane turned off the faucet before insinuating himself between Magnus and the kitchen sink. He threaded his fingers through Magnus' hair and pulled his head down. "Kiss me like you mean it."

Magnus closed the distance and pressed his lips against Dane's. He kept the kiss tame, using just the tip of his tongue to tease Dane's lower lip. *I want him.* The truth didn't surprise him, but the emotion behind it did. He wrapped his arms around Dane and took the kiss deeper, thrusting his tongue inside. *Make me feel normal*, he prayed.

Dane slid his hands down to untuck Magnus' T-shirt before slipping them underneath. Magnus groaned at the feel of Dane's touch. He broke the kiss long enough to pull his own shirt over his head. When he reached for Dane's he knew he wouldn't be satisfied until they were both naked. Of course, that would lead to fucking, which meant they would also need the supplies that were upstairs. *Shit.* What if Dane changed his mind again?

Before Magnus could voice his concerns, Dane leaned in and captured Magnus' nipple between his lips. The exquisite torture drove all thoughts of worry from Magnus' head. He directed Dane to the other nipple before going to work on Dane's jeans.

Dane bit down on the sensitive nub as he helped Magnus remove his jeans and underwear. There was something so erotic about having Dane naked from the waist down that Magnus couldn't keep himself from exploring. He fondled Dane's balls as he lowered his mouth for another kiss.

Working his way around Dane's hips, Magnus dipped his fingers in the hot dishwater before placing a warm finger against Dane's tight pucker.

"Oh God," Dane moaned, breaking the kiss. "So good."

Magnus repeated the process, slowly relaxing Dane's hole with the warmth. Dane hiked his leg up to wrap around the back of Magnus' legs, obviously needing more. Magnus hoisted Dane into his arms and settled him on the edge of the sink with his ass hanging over the side. Instead of dipping his fingers into the water, Magnus cupped his hand and thoroughly bathed the crack of Dane's ass.

Dane buried his face against Magnus' neck and held on tight, his body bucking as Magnus continued to play. "Fuck me," Dane begged.

They were the words Magnus had been waiting for. He grabbed Dane's ass and lifted him off the sink's edge. "Stuff's upstairs." As he headed out of the kitchen with Dane in his arms, Magnus' middle finger pushed deep inside Dane's hole. "You want my big cock instead of my finger?"

"Yes," Dane cried out, fucking himself on Magnus' finger.

"Not going to run away this time, are you?" Magnus took the stairs two at a time.

Dane shook his head as one of his hands found Magnus' distended nipple. He twisted the hard nub until Magnus' body began to shake. For years, Magnus had fucked men without feeling the level of need he currently battled.

By the time he reached the bedroom, Magnus could barely contain his desire. He threw Dane onto the bed and stripped his clothes with speed, bypassing finesse. Naked, Magnus reached down and repositioned Dane on his stomach, before tossing the supplies onto the mattress. The control he'd once prided himself on flew out of the window as Magnus buried his face against the crack of Dane's ass. He ran his tongue up and down the crevice several times before zeroing in on the soapy-tasting pucker.

"Magnus!" Dane screamed into the pillow under his head. He spread his legs farther apart and pushed against the invasion of Magnus' tongue.

Holy fuck! Magnus had never in his life been tempted to rim a person's ass. Yet, he couldn't seem to get enough. He slid a spit-drenched finger inside Dane's hole as he continued to flick his tongue against the puckered skin.

Dane began to writhe, as his whimpers grew louder. "Please fuck me."

Without taking his face away from Dane's ass, Magnus slid his finger out and reached for the supplies. Although he'd put on hundreds of condoms in his lifetime, the package in his hands proved difficult to open.

Forced to use his teeth, Magnus took one more swipe of Dane's hole with his tongue before sitting back on his haunches. He ripped open the foil packet despite his shaking hands, before rolling the condom down his throbbing length.

With his face still buried in the pillow, Dane reached back and separated the cheeks of his ass. Magnus dripped lube down Dane's crack, taking the time to make sure Dane was stretched enough to receive his cock. "Ready?" Magnus asked, tossing the bottle of lube onto the bed.

"Do it," Dane replied, his voice muffled by the pillow.

Magnus removed his fingers and directed the head of his cock to the stretched opening. As he did his best to take things slowly, he wiped the sweat from his forehead. He stared down at Dane's hole as it stretched to accommodate the intrusion. Dane's ass didn't look much different from the hundred or so others he'd fucked, so why did it feel so much sweeter as he pushed his way in?

A shiver travelled up Magnus' spine as he worked the last few inches inside Dane's ass. His body jerked at the pleasure, causing Dane to cry out.

"Give me a sec," Dane pleaded.

Magnus took the time to help Dane out of his shirt before running his hands up and down Dane's spine. The longer he waited for Dane's body to relax, the harder it became. He grabbed Dane's shirt off the bed where he'd tossed it and wiped the perspiration from his head and chest.

Several moments later, Dane wiggled his ass. "Sorry. It's been a while," Dane apologised.

Magnus withdrew his cock until only an inch or two remained inside before pushing back in. He found he quite liked the thought that Dane hadn't been with anyone else in a while. The feeling propelled him as he began to thrust in and out, each stroke harder than the last.

A feeling of possession began to overtake Magnus' need to remain aloof. He pulled his cock out of Dane's ass. "Turn around."

Dane glanced at Magnus over his shoulder. "You want me to suck your cock?"

Magnus grinned. "No, I want to fuck you face to face," he clarified.

A surprise expression crossed Dane's face. "Okay."

Magnus stared down at Dane as he changed positions. The dark bruise on Dane's neck spoke of possession, and Magnus found he quite enjoyed the thought of that. As he began to fuck Dane, he decided to mark Dane every day until they were forced to go back to their real lives.

Dane wrapped his legs around Magnus' waist and tried to pull him down. Before giving in to Dane's desire, Magnus took a moment to appreciate Dane's leanly muscled torso. The thought of twenty bruises marring the pale skin didn't sit well. As he lowered himself to lie on top of Dane, Magnus decided the bruise on Dane's neck would have to be the focus of his attention.

Dane's short fingernails bit into Magnus' back as the fucking continued. It seemed Magnus wasn't the only one who liked the idea of marking. When Magnus latched on to the bruised skin of Dane's neck and began to suck, Dane bucked.

The warmth Magnus felt between them signalled Dane's release. Free to reach for his own climax, Magnus pistoned his hips, driving his cock in and out of Dane's warm, tight hole.

Magnus' stroke lost its rhythm moments before he shot his first load of cum into the confines of the condom. A momentary dream of fucking without a condom flashed through his mind, fuelling another volley of seed.

By the time Dane's body had milked Magnus' cock dry, Magnus was exhausted. He collapsed to the side enough that he wasn't directly on top of Dane, but was still close enough to allow his cock to soften inside his hole.

As Magnus struggled to get his breathing under control, he shook off the idea of fucking without a condom. Never had he considered such a thing and the thought made him uncomfortable. He reached down and held the base of the condom as he withdrew his cock. In one smooth motion, Magnus tore off the rubber and climbed out of bed.

Magnus retreated to the hall bathroom without saying a word to Dane. He shut the door and twisted the old-fashioned key that stuck out of the lock. *What the hell is wrong with me?* He tossed the condom into the toilet before turning on the shower.

Heat of the moment, he tried to tell himself as he stepped into the shower. It had to be all the talk of James and the love he'd felt for his first wife. Somehow, the romantic notion that love really existed must've overwhelmed him. *Yeah, that has to be it.*

* * * *

Dane heard the shower and knew that Magnus wouldn't be back any time soon. He sat up and looked around the room, wondering what he was expected to do. Did he lie there and wait for Magnus to return or was he supposed to go back to his own room?

The possibility that Magnus already regretted their time together didn't bother Dane. Although Magnus might try to deny it, there had been a connection between them that had gone beyond the walls Magnus had built.

Dane slid out of bed and reached for his jeans. If Magnus needed time to come to the same conclusion, Dane would give it to him. He dressed quickly and left the room. As he passed the bathroom door, he couldn't help but smile. Let Magnus pretend he wanted nothing beyond a hard fuck. Dane knew the truth.

He rubbed the bruise on his neck, made even bigger by their recent entanglement. Dane doubted Magnus made a habit of giving his one-night stands hickeys. The thought thrilled him.

Instead of going to bed, Dane decided to head downstairs and finish the dishes. As he walked by the dining room table, he noticed his phone blinking, indicating he had a message. He grabbed it and continued on to the kitchen. After entering his passcode, he held the phone to his ear.

"It's Fallon. Give me a call as soon as you get this."

Dane started to panic. What if something had happened to his parents? He called his uncle and waited for him to answer.

"Hey," Fallon said.

"What's wrong?" Dane asked.

"I did some digging on your friend, and I don't like what I found," Fallon began.

"What?" Dane rubbed his bare chest. "You scared the shit out of me. I thought something bad had happened."

Fallon sighed. "Do you want to hear what I found out or not?" he asked, impatience in his voice.

"No, and I can't believe you had the nerve to dig into Magnus' background. Do you have all the men I'm interested in checked out?"

"Just the ones who are almost twice your age and in need of your connections to get what they want."

"Okay, first of all, Magnus is not twice my age, and, secondly, he didn't even know I was related to the Bennetts when he submitted that grant request."

"Bullshit. Someone like the Professor doesn't just willy-nilly turn in shit like that without doing some major research first. Hell, Dane, your name is on the fucking website. Do you really think he didn't see that?"

"What about the necklace I told you about?" Dane tried to argue. "I think if Mom had seen that she would've approved the grant without my okay."

"You've got no proof the necklace is authentic. All I'm saying is you need to be careful. The Professor's past is too shady for my comfort. Did he tell you his mom killed herself?"

Dane gasped, not out of shock, but out of sorrow. "I'm not discussing this with you. Why're you doing this?"

"Because I love you, and I refuse to stand by while this guy uses you," Fallon said.

"I love you, too, but I need you to stay out of this. Please. I grew up the rich kid, remember? I know what it feels like to be used and Magnus isn't doing that." In the past, Dane had felt loved by Fallon's overprotective nature, but he'd gone too far. "I'm hanging up now."

"Forget the wild goose chase he has you on and come to Austin," Fallon pleaded.

"I'm not going to Austin. I believe in Magnus, and I'm confident this is where I should be right now." Dane heard a noise and turned to find Magnus standing in the doorway. *Shit.* How much had he heard? "I'll talk to you later."

Dane hung up before Fallon could start another argument. "Hey," he said, setting his phone on the kitchen counter.

"Who was that?" Magnus asked.

"Uncle Fallon. He wants me to join the family in Austin for the holidays." Dane turned back to the sink and pulled the drain plug. "I thought I'd wash up these dishes before going to bed."

Dane held his breath, waiting for Magnus to say something. He set the plug back into the sink and began to refill it with hot water. Strong arms wrapped around him, causing him to jump.

"Easy," Magnus crooned.

"I didn't realise you were so close," he said in explanation. He squeezed a good amount of soap into the running water. "I thought you might need your space tonight."

Magnus kissed Dane's bare shoulder. "Quite honestly, I don't know what I need, but this feels nice."

Dane leant back against Magnus' chest, glad Magnus hadn't put on a shirt. There was something so incredibly sexy about a man with chest hair. He glanced down at his own hairless chest. It wasn't that he was one of those guys who waxed; Dane just happened to be from a family of hairless men. Oh, if he got right down to it and counted, he probably had about thirty short strands of blond hair, but they were virtually invisible against his skin.

Reaching around Dane, Magnus turned off the water and picked up one of the plates. He slowly washed the pale yellow china with Dane still pressed against him. "You're right. Doing dishes with someone else *is* more fun."

Dane reached to the side and pulled open the drawer with the dishtowels. He took the plate after Magnus gave it a quick rinse and dried it before setting it on the counter. Turning around, he began to kiss Magnus' jaw and neck. "How long do you think it'll take us to finish cleaning the kitchen at this rate?"

"Does it matter?" Magnus pulled his hands out of the dishwater and lowered Dane's zipper. "Was your uncle trying to warn you about me?"

Dane licked his lips. "He's protective."

Pushing his hand down the back of Dane's jeans, Magnus grunted. "I'm not after your money." He insinuated his middle finger deep into Dane's still-lubed hole. "I may not have as much as you do, but I make a damn good living for a kid from the south side of Chicago."

"Don't pay any attention to Fallon." Dane pressed his palms against Magnus' chest. "I'm here with you because I want to be. I may be young, but I'm not a fool."

Magnus removed his hand from Dane's pants and zipped him up. He stared into Dane's eyes as he brushed a soft kiss across his lips. "I've never lowered my walls enough to get to know a lover, but I think I'd like the chance with you. Would you care to sit out on the porch with me for a while?"

The request surprised Dane. Two minutes earlier they'd been well on their way to fucking again. He wondered what the sudden change in direction was about. "Sure. I'd like that."

Chapter Five

"Oh my God! What did you do?" Dane asked.

Magnus took his nose out of the book he was reading and smiled. Damn, Dane looked cute with sheet wrinkles still pressed into the side of his face. For days they'd poured over the research material found in the Institute, and although Magnus had found a few interesting articles, none of them mentioned the Native Americans who he believed had once shared the island. He noticed Dane looking at the stacks of books all around him. "Don't worry. I'll put 'em back."

"How're you going to remember what order they were in? There were three hundred and sixty-five books on those shelves."

"You know the exact number?"

"Of course. My mother once told me I could read a book a day and not finish for an entire year." Dane shrugged. "Of course, there might be one or two loaned out."

Magnus pulled his phone out of his pocket. "I took pictures of everything. Don't worry so much."

Dane sat cross-legged on the floor across from Magnus. "I have to admit, I wondered when you were going to discover this treasure trove."

Magnus ran his hand over the red leather cover of the book in his lap. "The books were all mixed together, but, as you can see, I sorted them by subject matter." He pointed towards the stacks of leather books. "The brown leather books are fiction, nothing really important there, but the rest are divided into interesting categories. Navy for Choctaw and black for government writings, including the Indian Removal Act of 1830." Magnus held up the red book in his hand. "Red, now that's where it gets interesting. Cherokee, Seminole, Chickasaw and Creek. All four represented under the same coloured binding. Why do you suppose James did that?"

Dane picked up one of the red books. "I've read all these, and I don't remember anything out of the ordinary in them other than the occasional screw-up by either the printer or the binder."

"No, me neither. Not yet anyway." Magnus added. He got to his feet and carried the book over to the sofa. "But I plan to get to every single one of them before I leave. It can't be a coincidence that the four nations represented in these red leather books are also found on the necklace."

Dane moved to sit across from Magnus in one of the wingback chairs.

"You don't want to sit beside me?" Magnus had become used to Dane's presence over the last five days. Actually, he'd come to enjoy his assistant's company both day and night.

"We both know if I sit over there we won't get any reading done." Dane chuckled. "Maybe we can take a study break later."

"Yeah, maybe." Magnus opened the book and continued reading where he'd left off when Dane had come into the library. So far, the book hadn't contained any new information, but Magnus knew there had to be a reason James Barrett had spent so much money to have them bound in special leather covers.

Halfway through the book, he stopped reading and flipped to the next page. "That's weird," Magnus mumbled.

"What? Did you find something?" Dane asked.

"Not really. This page doesn't fit in with the rest of the book. I'm reading about the Seminole and suddenly it starts talking about the Cherokees."

Dane nodded his head. "Yeah, I've run across that problem before in these books. I think whoever rebound them screwed up. I'm sure there's a book somewhere that's missing half its pages, but I've never run across it."

Magnus glanced at the stacks of books. "Are you just talking about the red ones?"

"No. I remember reading *The Adventures of Tom Sawyer* when I was young and suddenly there was a page I didn't understand at all." Dane bit his bottom lip before shaking his head. "I can't remember what it was, but I remember asking my mom about it at the time. She told me not to worry about it; that mistakes happen but it shouldn't ruin a perfectly good story." He stood and went over to the stack of brown leather books. "It should be here."

Magnus thought about what Dane had said. "What if there's another book hidden *within* these books?"

Dane tried to get a book out of the stack and ended up toppling a number of volumes onto the library floor. "Oops," he said, looking at the mess he'd made. He carried a book over and sat beside Magnus. "I have no idea where that page is, but I'll find it."

Magnus marked his place with a receipt from his wallet before reaching for another book. He began flipping through the pages, looking for any inconsistencies.

"Here it is." Dane handed the book of *Tom Sawyer* over to Magnus.

The first thing Magnus looked at was the page number. Although, according to the rest of the book, the page was in the proper order, it definitely wasn't part of the story. He began to read the page. The sentence structure was definitely broken English with Muskegon thrown in. "It reads like a diary, but there are big gaps in the sentences like words have been removed before it was printed."

Magnus tried to piece together the gist of the text. "Basically, it's talking about a tribe who agreed to sacrifice themselves for the good of the Indian nation that would rise after them."

"They killed themselves?" Dane asked, scooting closer.

Magnus shook his head. "I don't think it's meant to be taken literally. See this word?" He pointed towards the page. "*Ushta* is the Choctaw word for four. Whoever wrote this had to be Choctaw, and we both know they were among the first to comply with the Indian Removal Act. Supposedly, they relocated willingly, something I never understood, but maybe that was the *sacrifice* the author talks about."

Magnus glanced at the stacks of books all around him. "We need to go through every one of these. Is there a printer in here?"

Dane shook his head. "No, but there are several big ones at the Institute."

The responsibility of transferring an entire library of rare and expensive books was absurd. "Can we borrow a printer and bring it here?"

"I don't see why not." Dane moved to straddle Magnus' lap. "But maybe we could take a short study break first."

Magnus captured Dane's mouth in an all-consuming kiss. As excited as he was to delve into the books, holding Dane in his arms had become an addiction. It was wreaking havoc on the fortress he'd built around his heart, but for now he planned to enjoy every moment of their time together.

* * * *

After a day and a half of searching through books, Dane's eyes felt like they were about to fall out of his head. He leant back in the rocking chair and put the phone to his ear. He loved the view from the veranda outside James' bedroom, always had.

"Hey, stranger," Bobby answered.

"You're stranger than I am," Dane teased his friend. "How's Ares?"

"I think he's in love with the poodle next door. I keep telling him it's not in the cards, but he isn't listening." Bobby laughed.

"Poor Ares. It seems we're both destined to love someone we can't have." Dane closed his eyes and leaned his head against the back of the chair.

"Shit. So it's not going well?"

"The opposite. It's going too well. He keeps telling me we should enjoy our time together and not worry about the future, but I can't think of anything else." A noise from inside the house caught Dane's attention. "Hang on a sec," he told Bobby.

Dane walked through the French doors to find Magnus, his hair in total disarray, pulling drawers out of the dresser. "What're you doing?"

"I found a page that..." Magnus stopped talking and pointed towards the phone in Dane's hand. "Who are you talking to?"

"Bobby. I'll finish up." Dane turned away from Magnus and spoke into the phone. "I need to go. Will you be home later?"

"Not tonight. We're going to the annual Christmas party at Justin and Luc's place," Bobby said. "But you can call me tomorrow afternoon. Let me repeat that, afff terrr nooon."

"Got it. Have fun at the party. Tell Chet I said hi." Dane hung up the phone and stuck it in his pocket. "Sorry, now, tell me why you're destroying the dresser?"

"I'm not destroying anything." Magnus held up one of the drawers showing Dane that it was intact. "There's a page in one of the books that talks about James sleeping with secrets."

Dane looked around the room. "Then it has to be in the bed."

Magnus stood and walked over to the huge custom-made bed. "Help me with the mattress."

The thought of Magnus tearing apart the bed didn't sit well with Dane. "Hang on, let's think about this."

"You're the one who said it was probably in the bed."

"I know, but destroying a one-of-a-kind antique isn't the answer." Dane began to explore the large bedposts. "Maybe there's a hidden panel or something."

Magnus joined Dane in the search, working on the opposite side of the bed. "Come on, be here, damn it," Magnus said, dropping to his knees.

For a brief moment Dane thought he'd found something, but it turned out to be just a small split in the mahogany. Once he'd searched the first one without luck, he moved to the next post. "Can I ask you something?"

Magnus stood and walked towards the head of the bed. "Sure."

"You've been acting kinda funny all day. Did you find something you're not telling me about?" Dane asked.

Magnus stared at Dane for several moments before sitting on the edge of the mattress. "I've been piecing the pages together and I think I've got a pretty clear idea of what happened, but I need proof."

"So, what's the story?" Despite his education, it all seemed so unreal to Dane. The island had always been a place to come together with his family and embrace their heritage, not a place of mystery.

"Four nations sent their best warriors to this island."

"Why?" Dane dropped down beside Magnus.

"I believe they had a plan to band together and rebuild their numbers. Remember the passage in *Tom Sawyer*. The Choctaw vowed to sacrifice themselves for the four who would come together and rise again."

"To fight the government? Do you think they really believed they could succeed?"

Magnus shrugged. "What choice did they have? The government ordered them off their land. They were warriors ordered to live on a piece of dry land in Oklahoma."

Dane reached for Magnus' hand. The passion behind the words touched him. "Would you have fought?"

Magnus squeezed Dane's hand. "Yes. I would. Does that surprise you?"

"Not at all." Turning to sit sideways, Dane studied Magnus for several moments. "Did you have to fight to get out of Chicago?"

Magnus' spine stiffened. "I don't talk about that."

"I know, but maybe you should." Dane knew he was pushing. He just hoped like hell he wouldn't regret it.

Magnus stood. "Why? You think if I cry on your shoulder the past will magically be wiped away? It doesn't work like that. *I* don't work like that."

Before Dane could respond, Magnus stormed from the room. "Shit." Dane started to go after him, but changed his mind. He spun around and looked at the portrait above the fireplace. His gaze immediately went to the rock in the background. "Do you want your secret told?"

Dane wasn't sure James wanted the public to know. James had gone to great lengths to have the story of the Native Americans hidden in his personal library. The leather-bound books downstairs hadn't been integrated into the Institute's vast library because of a request in James Bennett's will that the house remain intact.

"Give me a sign that you wanted us to uncover your secrets?" he whispered.

Dane continued to stare at the painting. Instead of looking straight at the artist who'd painted the portrait, James Bennett's head was turned in profile. Dane followed James' line of sight, which landed squarely on the bed. "It has to be there," he whispered.

Moving to stand at the end of the bed, Dane studied the ornately carved headboard. He climbed onto the bed and began to run his hands over the wood. "Oh, shit."

The massive piece of wood did indeed hold a secret. One of the reliefs in the carved detailing held an actual key. Dane jumped off the bed and grabbed a letter opener from the small writing desk in front of the window. He glanced up at the painting. "Forgive me."

It took several moments, but Dane managed to work the key free of its hiding place with only minimal damage to the bed. Although the key fitted in the palm of his hand, the weight went beyond a physical measurement.

"I'm taking the boat across the creek. You coming?" Magnus asked from behind Dane.

Dane dropped the letter opener among the pillows before Magnus spotted it. Why he was holding back the discovery Dane had no idea, except he needed time to process the newest development. Still, the small strip of land wasn't a safe place to wander around alone. "Let me get one of the guns from downstairs first."

"Guns? You expecting someone?"

"Snakes, alligators, take your pick. I told you, that land hasn't been maintained for years."

Magnus chuckled. "Do you honestly think I'd trust you with a gun?"

Dane took a deep calming breath when his hackles rose. It wasn't often he lost his temper, but his moments of rage were still discussed at the Thanksgiving table.

"Yeah, I don't think so," Magnus said, an irritating smirk on his otherwise handsome face.

"Shut the fuck up!" Dane exploded. "When will you get it through your thick skull that I'm not the enemy? And I'm sick of you treating me like I'm worthless. For your information, I started taking pot shots at frogs when I was five, the year I received my first bb gun." Dane pushed past Magnus and out of the room.

As torn as he was between helping Magnus discover the truth and keeping it buried, the last thing he was in the mood for was Magnus' ongoing mistrust. He went to his room and pulled his suitcases out of the closet.

"What're you doing?" Magnus asked from the doorway.

"Leaving," Dane stated. "I know I begged you to bring me here, but it doesn't feel right any more. I don't feel right about what we're doing."

"I don't want you to leave, but I need you to tell me why you're questioning the project."

"I've wanted to be an anthropologist since I was in junior high. I always thought it would be exciting to find out about people and cultures from our past, but now..." Dane shook his head. "It feels intrusive. Look at it this way, you obviously have a lot of secrets; how would you feel if, years from now, someone started poking around in your life?"

Magnus shook his head. "This has nothing to do with my past. I think we've discovered something incredibly important to the Native American people."

"But it obviously didn't work. I don't know what happened here, but does the world really need to know those tribes sacrificed their best warriors for nothing?"

"Don't forget the passage. The Choctaw were meant to remember. Now, I don't know why they didn't, but we're only doing what those four tribes wanted in the first place."

Dane could see he wasn't going to deter Magnus. If he stayed, he'd at least have some control over the situation. His need to protect his family was becoming increasingly more important. A thought struck him. He wondered if his mom and uncle knew the secrets to be found at Barrett House. "Would you give me a few minutes to get myself together?"

Magnus cupped the back of Dane's head in his hand and leaned in for a soft kiss. "I'm sorry about earlier, but I meant what I said. I really don't want you to leave."

Dane nodded. "We've been working hard the last few days. Maybe we're due for a break. Can I interest you in a picnic?"

"Yeah, that might be a good idea. I'll go throw together some of the fried chicken left over from last night."

"Sounds good." Dane accepted another kiss from Magnus. "I'll be down in a few minutes."

After Magnus left the room, Dane pulled out his cell phone.

"Were your ears burning?" Evelyn Jefferson asked.

"Hi, Mom. No, but now you've spilled the beans. Why were you talking about me?"

"Fallon and I were discussing the fact that you'd rather be at Bennett House playing anthropologist than here with us," she explained.

"I'm not playing at anything, and quite frankly it hurts that you would even say that to me." Maybe it had been a mistake to call home.

"I'm sorry, baby. You're right, that was uncalled for."

"Thanks," Dane mumbled. He pulled the key out of his pocket and stared at it. "Mom, I need to know something."

"Okay."

"You know the reason Professor Sofokleous and I are here, don't you?"

"Why do you ask?"

"Because I think you gave me Magnus' grant request for a reason and I want to know what it is."

"I told you at the time you were the best person to approve or reject it. I haven't changed my mind about that. We trusted you. We still do."

"You know, don't you?"

His mother's silence confirmed what he'd begun to suspect. "We don't have any real proof yet, but Magnus is like a dog with a bone right now. He's not going to give up until he finds what he's looking for. So, if this is something I'm supposed to sabotage, I need to know. Now."

Evelyn sighed. "I can't tell you what to do. I asked you to approve the proposal because your uncle and I have had our suspicions for years but could never find anything to prove it. I know if anyone could do that, it would be you and your professor."

"So you want me to continue?"

"Yes."

"And what should I do if we find the proof?"

"Whatever it is you find, we trust you to do the right thing," Evelyn said.

"No pressure there." He returned the key to his pocket.

"It may turn out we're worried about nothing, but we both find it strange there isn't any evidence that

Native Americans ever occupied the island. It's as if all trace of them has been hidden."

"Except the pages in the books. Why leave those?" Dane asked.

"I don't know," Evelyn confessed. "I guess that's part of what you need to figure out."

It was Dane's turn to sigh. "It's a little too cloak and dagger for me, Mom." How did he explain to her that all he'd wanted was to spend time alone with Magnus? "I have to tell Magnus."

"Yes, Fallon told me he noticed something between the two of you. Just don't let it get in the way."

"Get in the way? You make it sound like my feelings aren't as important as the stupid secrets on this island."

Evelyn cleared her throat. "I love you, baby, but I know Fallon's already warned you about what type of man you're falling for."

"Yeah, and I'll tell you the same thing I told him. Butt out. You want me to do this, fine, but I'll do it on my terms." Dane hung up and turned off his phone. He had a picnic to attend and he damn well planned to enjoy it.

* * * *

Magnus watched as Dane started to lick the chicken grease off his fingers. "Here, let me do that," he said, grabbing Dane's hand. He closed his lips around Dane's thumb and sucked.

"Mmm," Dane moaned. "You're going to make me fall."

Magnus withdrew Dane's thumb and looked down from the giant tree limb they were perched on. "We're, like, four feet off the ground."

"I could still get hurt," Dane mumbled, sticking his pointer finger between Magnus' lips.

One by one, Magnus cleaned each of Dane's digits, taking the time to tickle between them with the tip of his tongue.

"You're making me hard, and I need to talk to you about something."

Magnus moved to straddle the tree limb. "Show me how hard you are." He reached for Dane's button fly. "Zippers are much faster."

Dane turned to mirror Magnus' position on the limb. "I didn't know it was a race."

Magnus eased the last button out of its hole before reaching inside for Dane's cock. "This is my kind of picnic. Slow and easy," he said, stroking Dane's erection.

As Dane thrust against Magnus' hand, he started to fall sideways, his arms searching for anything to hold on to. Acting quickly, Magnus reached out and grabbed Dane's forearm. "Easy there, Monkey," he said, using Dane's childhood nickname.

Dane was the first to laugh. "If you ever try to jack me off while I'm sitting in a tree again, I'll feed you to the 'gators."

Laughing, Magnus hopped to the ground and pulled Dane down into his arms. "'Gators, huh?"

Dane snapped, catching the skin of Magnus' neck between his teeth. The harder Dane sucked, the hornier Magnus became. It didn't seem to matter how many times he told himself not to let Dane into his solitary world, Magnus couldn't bring himself to push Dane away. He'd even begun to consider a relationship beyond their time in Louisiana. Which was completely inappropriate and broke every rule he'd ever had, but, oh, the longer Dane sucked on his neck, the more Magnus yearned for more.

"There, now I've marked *you*," Dane said, inspecting his work. He tilted his head back. "It's darker than mine."

Magnus ran his tongue over the deep bruise. He'd made sure to suck on that bit of skin each morning since they'd started sleeping together. "I doubt anything could be as dark as this one." He licked the bruise again before setting Dane on his feet. "Since you won't let me jack you off in the tree, could I interest you in a stroll back to the house?"

Dane rested his forehead against Magnus' shoulder. "I think there's some kind of bug crawling down my dick."

Without thought, Magnus sank to his knees and began to inspect Dane's half-hard cock. "I don't see any bugs, but I see a spot that needs some attention." Magnus licked Dane's cock from base to tip, slipping his lips over the head. The velvety soft skin against his tongue was a rare occurrence, but one he thought he'd like to get used to as long as it was Dane's cock he was blowing.

Dane ran his fingers through Magnus' hair. "I haven't had anyone do that in years."

Magnus held Dane's cock by the base and tapped it against his lips. "Good. Let's pretend you've never had someone do this to you."

"Fine by me." Dane moaned and thrust his hips when Magnus took him back into his mouth.

Magnus did his best to open his throat, but he wasn't used to the invasion and choked. Embarrassed, he glanced up at Dane. "Sorry."

When he tried to put Dane's cock back into his mouth, Dane shook his head and took a step back, pulling his cock out of Magnus' reach. "You don't have to do that."

"Maybe I want to."

Dane smiled and stuffed his cock back into his underwear. "There are times when I see glimpses of the man behind the walls and it breaks my heart because I wish I could keep him."

Magnus got to his feet. As much as he wanted to tell Dane otherwise, he could never be less than honest. "We have a week left. Don't spoil it by hoping for things that can't happen."

"Why is it so bad to date a student? Hell, I'll quit if I need to. I can get another job, find another school. I'll do whatever it takes if it means I don't have to say goodbye to you."

Magnus stared at Dane, trying to figure out what to say. Promises were hollow words easily broken. He prided himself on telling the truth, but had no idea if the truth would help or hurt the situation. "Come back to the house with me," he said instead.

Dane hesitated, but eventually nodded. "Sooner or later we need to talk about this."

"I know." Magnus did know. Unfortunately, he still wasn't sure if he was even capable of letting someone in.

Chapter Six

Three days later, they were back on the small strip of land across the water from the Barrett House. With a rifle carried safely under his arm, Dane climbed out of the small rowboat. It wasn't exactly the way he'd hoped to spend Christmas Eve, but their time on the island was short. "Do you really think we'll find something this time?" They'd already made two trips across the water, only to come up with nothing. Well, except Magnus had literally squealed when he'd kicked a hollow log and a snake had slithered out. Needless to say, Magnus had been all for Dane bringing the rifle on this trip.

The thick undergrowth snagged Dane's boots as he tried to keep up with Magnus. "From what I've heard, the centre of the island used to be a big flower garden. Sad that it's been neglected for so long."

"What else was here?" Magnus asked, a shovel resting on his shoulder.

"I don't know. It's been this way since I was a boy." Dane stepped on a rock and bent to check it out before continuing.

"I'd like to search this area," Magnus said, stabbing the blade of the shovel into the ground.

"Okay. I'll just go over there and get started." Dane set the rifle against a log and took the pack off his back. He dug inside and pulled out a collapsible shovel. After two days of digging, his hands were sore and blistered. He glanced at Magnus before retrieving a pair of gloves from his backpack.

Three hours later, they'd yet to find even a single item. "Maybe we should look somewhere else," Dane suggested.

"This is the highest point. If anything survived the floods, it would be here," Magnus countered.

"Yeah, but maybe when the water receded it carried something closer to the waterline." It made sense to Dane, but Magnus didn't appear to agree.

"Go ahead and give it a try if you want, but I think I might be close to something here." Magnus turned back to the wide hole he'd been working on, leaving Dane to dig where he pleased.

"Did you find something?" Dane asked, taking off his gloves.

Magnus paused and shook his head. "Not yet, but I will."

Dane looked around the area. He couldn't explain it, but he felt in his bones they wouldn't find anything. The land was too narrow to live on, and every bit of information he had said that the strip had been used for planting. His gaze went to the Bennett House, a pale yellow monument in the centre of the plantation. Dane picked up the rifle and walked over to Magnus. "If I leave the rifle here, would you mind if I go back to the house? I'd like to try searching around there again."

In reality, the key was burning a hole in his pocket. He felt like a Grade A asshole for not telling Magnus about it. Hell, he felt like a double agent, but his family loyalty continued to play heavily on his conscience.

Magnus glanced at Dane's hands and winced. "Yeah, it might be better for you to take a break." He held up his own hands. "After years in the field, my hands are practically indestructible."

Dane leaned over and kissed Magnus' dirty palm. "They're fantastic hands."

Magnus chuckled. "I'm glad you think so." He wrapped one arm around Dane's waist and pulled him into a deep kiss. "I'll be back by dinner."

"How? You won't have a boat. Give me a call when you're ready, and I'll come back and get you."

"You don't want me to swim for it?" Magnus joked.

"In that stagnant water? I don't think so." After another kiss, Dane handed Magnus the rifle. "Safety's on, but make sure you don't point it at anything you don't want to kill."

"Gun safety one-oh-one?"

Dane kissed Magnus' cheek. "Something like that. Just stay safe."

After a quick trip across the dark water, Dane docked the boat. Instead of going to the house, he soon found himself in the cemetery. "It's here," he whispered to himself. If there was proof, it had to be in the cemetery.

Dane stared at the statue. "The loss of one's soul forever changes the beauty of the landscape," Dane read the words again. The likeness of James Bennett faced the mausoleum. Not only did the statue not face the cemetery entrance, but its back was turned. It had to mean something, but what?

Squatting beside the statue's base, Dane began to examine the plaque. He pressed against each corner, half expecting some secret passage to pop open and reveal the answers to all their questions.

It soon became clear that the only way to find out what—if anything—was inside the base was to destroy it. He lay on his back and stared up at James Bennett. The passage in the book played through his mind. Dane shook his head. There were too many clues, too damn many riddles.

"Where do I start?" he asked the statue. Did he destroy the statue only to find nothing inside? What about the bed? How many family heirlooms would be destroyed trying to find something that may not even exist?

"Damn it," he said, getting to his feet.

Dane walked into the caretaker's shed and searched until he came up with a sledgehammer and a crowbar. He stared at the tools in his hands and wondered if he had the guts to go through with it. The statue was made of bronze, so, other than a few dings, he felt sure it could be remounted; at least he hoped so.

Returning to the statue, Dane's first swing with the sledgehammer was less than impressive, maybe because his heart wasn't in it. He glanced towards the strip of land that his heart presently occupied.

For years he'd fancied himself in love with Professor Sofokleous, but those feelings couldn't hold a candle to the way he felt about Magnus now. Hero worship and pure lust would best describe his attraction to his professor only two weeks ago, but that was before he'd seen the look of fear in Magnus' eyes each time he let his guard down. Before he'd heard the deep timbre of Magnus' laugh while he watched late-night cartoons when he thought no one else was in the room, and before he'd gazed into the dark brown depths of Magnus' eyes as they made love.

The thought of pretending he didn't love Magnus when they left Louisiana fuelled Dane's strength as he swung the sledgehammer again. "Stupid rules!" he screamed.

The head of the hammer connected to the aging Portland cement, sending small chips flying back at him. Despite the slight sting to his cheek, the physical outlet for his anger felt exhilarating. He swung again, and again, putting all his frustration into destroying a piece of the plantation's history.

By the time his strength and anger had left him, a sizeable hole in the cement base had been created. He dropped the sledgehammer and collapsed to the debris-laden grass. His elbow connected with a sharp piece of cement, but Dane barely felt it as his gaze landed on the etched rock he'd spent years searching for. "No wonder I couldn't find it."

Dane reached inside to move the rock and hit something hidden behind it. Unable to see what it was, he hit it again with the back of his hand. A hollow metal sound answered him.

With his heart beating rapidly, Dane worked the rock out of the way an inch at a time. When he saw the metal box for the first time, Dane drew his hands back as if the container was dangerous, and in a way it could be.

Dane continued to stare at the box. Finding proof meant there would be no going back. Worse, it meant he'd have to tell Magnus that he'd kept him in the dark about the key. He took a deep breath and grabbed the box.

Like the wimp he was, Dane tucked the box under his arm and ran towards the house. He didn't even bother cleaning up his mess, something his mom would be horrified over. *I'll do it later*, he promised himself.

Dane went straight to the bathroom and locked the door. The moment he realised what he'd done he started to laugh. His adolescence had been spent behind the locked door of a bathroom, trying to make himself feel something for the women in the magazine that his friend had given him. His junior year of high school he'd stumbled across Fallon's hidden stash of porn. After trying to wipe the thought of his uncle pleasuring himself to the naked male bodies in the magazines, Dane had wasted no time swiping a few for himself. It had been the beginning of a very busy few years.

He glanced at himself in the mirror. A small trail of dried blood marked his cheek where the flying debris had caught him. Dane wondered for a brief moment if it made him look tough.

He glanced at the box sitting on the edge of the sink. Yeah, tough. He was so afraid of what might be in the box he was daydreaming about his first jerk-off session.

Dane jumped when his cell phone began to ring. He reached into his pocket and brushed the key with his finger as he grabbed his phone. "Hello?"

"I'm ready whenever you are," Magnus said.

Dane glanced at the box. "Did you find anything?"

"Not yet," Magnus confessed. "But I'm not giving up."

Of course not. Magnus wouldn't be the man Dane had fallen in love with if he let himself get discouraged so easily. "I'll be right there."

"I'll dig another ten minutes and meet you at the dock."

Magnus hung up, leaving Dane alone in the bathroom with a secret that could potentially blow up in his face.

* * * *

As Dane neared the dock, Magnus noticed the small cut on his cheek. Concern for Dane struck Magnus like a bolt of lightning. "What happened?"

Dane touched his cheek. "Nothing. Just a nick."

Magnus handed Dane the rifle before climbing into the boat. He examined the cut for himself. "How'd it happen?" He brushed his thumb around the half-inch-long injury.

Dane leaned into Magnus' touch. "You know me, I'm a klutz, always have been."

How many times had Magnus witnessed Dane's less than smooth moves? "You should be more careful." He pushed the boat away from the dock and took control of the oars. A few hours earlier it had dawned on Magnus that Dane was sacrificing Christmas Eve with his family in order to help him.

"I'll cook tonight," he offered. The movement stirred the air around him, making him wince. "Right after I wash the stink off."

Dane tapped his foot against Magnus'. "I don't mind a little sweat."

"Yeah, well neither do I, but I'm way beyond just being sweaty. I reek."

Dane wrinkled his nose. "Now that you mention it..."

Magnus laughed. Moments like this had him questioning his resolve to end their affair before leaving the island. It wasn't Dane that was holding him back; it was Magnus' fear of letting him in.

They made the short trek across the stream and tied off the boat. "So what've you been up to all afternoon?" Magnus asked.

Dane turned away and began to empty the rifle of its bullets. When he'd finished, he stuck the ammunition in his pocket. Withdrawing his hand, Dane stretched out his arm, his fist closed tight. "I found this."

Magnus stepped forward and held his palm open. "What is it?"

Dane dropped a small, cool object into Magnus' hand. "I found it in the headboard of the bed."

Magnus held the key up for closer inspection. "Was it hidden?"

"Yeah, it was stuck in one of the deep grooves."

Magnus' worry that he'd wasted time digging and refilling holes for three days faded to the back of his mind as he stared at the key. "So, the passage in the papers was right; James was sleeping with secrets."

He started up the crushed shell walkway, hoping Dane would follow. Magnus wasn't blind; he could tell there was something bothering Dane. He'd definitely got the feeling Dane didn't like digging. At first Magnus thought it was the actual work involved, but it soon became apparent it was more.

Magnus tried to put himself in Dane's position. The Bennett family had to be proud of the Institute and all it had accomplished in the study of Native American history. Since neither of them knew what kind of information they might uncover, it was natural for Dane to worry. He turned around and walked back to Dane. "What we're doing is important."

Dane nodded when Magnus wrapped an arm around him. "Yeah."

With his hand resting on Dane's shoulder from behind, Magnus was able to get Dane moving towards the house. "James wouldn't have left the clues if he didn't want someone to find them."

Dane's head lowered. "That's what I keep telling myself." He sighed. "But, if that's the case, why hide the proof in the first place?"

"I don't know. Maybe we'll find something to explain his reasoning behind it all." Magnus kissed Dane's temple. Although it went against his usual work ethic on a dig, Magnus felt it was important for them to take a step back for an evening. "Enough shop talk for now. Let's take a break and enjoy Christmas Eve."

Dane finally wrapped his arm around Magnus' waist, hooking his thumb into Magnus' belt loop. "You want company in the shower?"

Surprised by the request, Magnus misjudged the first porch step and nearly sent them both tumbling. He caught his balance and managed to hang on to Dane at the same time. He'd never showered with a lover. In his opinion, it was more intimate than fucking. However, oddly enough, he found the suggestion appealing. "I think I'd like that."

* * * *

Magnus used his size to shield the spray from hitting Dane in the face. "Better?"

Dane grinned and reached for the liquid soap. "Much, although I'll probably freeze now."

Magnus wrapped both arms around Dane and pulled him against his chest. "How's that?"

"Well, I'm warmer, but it makes it harder to get you clean." He broke free of Magnus' embrace and took a step back. "It's okay. I don't mind the cold as long as I can do this." With those words, Dane began to run his hands over Magnus' chest.

Magnus reached for the shampoo to wash his hair, but Dane took the bottle out of his hand. "Please let me do it." He set the shampoo out of Magnus' reach. "Your hair drives me crazy, especially now since it's grown out. The thought of running my fingers through it is enough to keep me warm."

Magnus had meant to get it cut before winter break had started. The last week or so, he hadn't been able to keep the curls from forming. "I don't like it curly."

"Why?" Dane ran his soapy hands under Magnus' arms to thoroughly wash his armpits.

Did Magnus dare tell Dane the truth? He could just as easily make up a lie, but staring down into those big trusting eyes, he couldn't do it. "My mom liked the curls too, so she rarely cut my hair. Unfortunately, my hair was the first thing my father reached for when he was angry with me. I've kept it cut short since I left home."

Dane reached for the bottle and squeezed shampoo into his palm. "Let me show you what it feels like to have someone touch your hair out of love rather than anger." He reached up and began to work the shampoo into Magnus' hair.

Magnus watched Dane closely, wary of the gentle massage. Although Dane had said he was touching him out of love, Magnus knew it was impossible. Love didn't really exist, not in the way Hollywood portrayed it anyway. Sure, his parents had spoken of love once their fights were over. It was always right before they disappeared into the bedroom for hours. But soon enough the name calling would begin again. If that was love, Magnus wanted no part of it; never had. His mom had told him she loved him on occasion, yet didn't even like him enough to make sure he was fed.

"Does that feel good?" Dane asked.

Magnus admitted to himself that he hadn't taken the time to process what the massage was making him feel. He'd been too busy questioning the motive behind Dane's actions. "It's okay," he finally said.

Dane's blond eyebrows drew together. "Then I'm doing something wrong."

Magnus shook his head. "It's not you. It's me." He rested his hands on Dane's shoulders. "I told you, I don't trust people enough to let them in."

Dane stared up at Magnus for several moments. "Let's get you rinsed off. There's something I need to show you."

While Magnus rinsed the shampoo from his hair, Dane quickly washed his own hair. Once Magnus was finished, he reached for the liquid soap and began to wash Dane's body. He worked efficiently until he reached Dane's cock and balls.

Dane moaned, and the joy of showering with someone became clear to Magnus for the first time in his life. Dane didn't try to hide his need for more, and Magnus went further. He wrapped one hand around Dane's erection while the other sought Dane's puckered hole. The slick soap made entrance easy as he slipped a finger inside.

"Magnus," Dane moaned as he began to ride Magnus' hand. Dane's eyes closed, and Magnus understood what having the right kind of control over someone's pleasure felt like. His cock hardened as he continued to please Dane. He'd searched his entire life for the pleasure he was suddenly experiencing for the first time.

Magnus added a second finger to Dane's hole. With a gasp, Dane opened his eyes. "I'm coming," Dane said, moments before Magnus' hand was covered in the warmth of Dane's seed.

The trust evident in Dane's expression pushed Magnus over the edge. The moment was so incredibly pure that Magnus came with little stimulation to his own cock. As he gave in to the emotions pounding against the thick wall around his heart, Magnus realised his life would never be the same.

He buried his hands in Dane's wet hair and tilted his head up. Speech wasn't possible because he had no words to describe what he felt. Instead, he tried to convey his new-found feelings in a deep kiss.

The cooling water eventually broke the two apart. "Thank you," Dane whispered against Magnus' lips.

"I'm the one who should thank you," Magnus answered in return. He shut off the water and grabbed the two towels off the bar beside the shower. "I might need a nap before I make dinner."

Dane smiled and began to dry off. "First, there's something I need to give you." He wrapped the towel around his waist and left the room.

Magnus quickly followed suit. "You don't have to give it to me now," he said, going after Dane.

Standing in the doorway of his room, Dane paused. "Yeah, I think I do," he said without turning to look at Magnus.

Dane continued into the room and pulled his suitcase out of the closet.

Magnus' heart skipped a beat. "Are you leaving?"

Dane set the suitcase on the bed and began to unzip it. "No, not unless you ask me to." He opened the piece of expensive luggage and pulled out something wrapped in a towel. Instead of giving it to Magnus,

Dane hugged it against his chest and sat on the edge of the bed. "I found this today. I'm sorry I didn't tell you about it earlier, but I felt it was important to look at it first."

"And did you?" Magnus asked, stunned at the revelation.

"No. I haven't even tried to open it yet." Dane looked up at Magnus. "I'm afraid of what might be inside."

"Why?" Magnus entered the room. He lifted the empty suitcase to the floor before taking a seat beside Dane.

"Because once I know I can't unknow." He shook his head. "That probably doesn't make any sense to someone like you."

"What do you mean, someone like me?" Magnus' hackles began to rise.

"You see the world in black and white. Finding out the mystery behind this plantation is a quest, a job for you. But for me it's family history; that's my grey area."

As much as Magnus wanted to argue the dissection of his personality, he found he couldn't. Dane was right: in his opinion, history was meant to be shared, the good and the bad. "We'll open it together," he said. It was all he could promise at the moment.

Dane handed Magnus the wrapped package. The key in the pocket of his jeans no doubt unlocked the secret treasure. "I'll be right back," Magnus said. He handed the box back to Dane before returning to the bathroom to retrieve the key out of his jeans' pocket.

As anxious as he was to open the box, Magnus knew it was something Dane should do. He sat on the bed and handed Dane the key. "You do it."

Dane stared at Magnus for several moments before shaking his head. "Actually, I think I'd rather you did it. If it's something bad, I don't want to know. So, I'm going to go downstairs and start dinner."

Dane leaned over and gave Magnus a quick kiss before climbing off the bed. He gathered a clean change of clothes and left the room without taking time to get dressed.

Magnus fitted the key into the lock and tried to turn it, but nothing happened. Even though the key seemed to fit, the lock was so rusted the mechanics were probably all seized up. He'd need to break the lock in order to see what was inside. Strangely, Magnus thought of Dane and how it would make him feel if the box was broken.

Box in hand, Magnus returned to his room to get dressed. It dawned on him that he hadn't asked Dane where he'd found the treasure. After pulling on a pair of jeans and a T-shirt, Magnus carried the box downstairs. He entered the kitchen to find Dane seated at the small kitchen table. "You okay?"

Dane shrugged. "What'd you find?"

"Nothing yet. The lock's rusted shut. I'll need a screwdriver and hammer to open it, but I thought I'd check with you first."

"The box itself isn't important. Do what you have to."

"Okay." He glanced around the room. "Do you know where I can find a toolbox?"

Dane stood and opened the door to the large walk-in pantry. He was back in a few moments with an old red toolbox, which he handed to Magnus. "Should I grill those steaks for dinner or would you rather have the ham?"

Normally, Magnus would've told Dane it didn't matter, but it was apparent Dane needed something to keep himself busy while Magnus investigated the box. "If you made the ham, we could eat the leftovers tomorrow instead of cooking."

"Good idea."

Magnus set the tools and old metal box on the floor before pulling Dane into his arms. "Would you rather I open this tomorrow?"

"I can't ask you to do that."

"You didn't ask, I offered. Whatever secrets that box contains have been hidden for over a hundred and fifty years. I don't think another day is going to matter."

Dane tightened his embrace. "In that case, yeah, I think I'd rather have at least one more night with you."

Magnus stepped back and stared down at Dane. "What's that supposed to mean? You think just because I find the answers I've been looking for I won't want you anymore?"

Dane placed his hands on Magnus' chest. "I think whatever's in that box might tear us apart even before we return to Idaho."

For some reason, Dane's words sounded like a challenge to Magnus. Anger filled him as he opened the toolbox and removed a standard screwdriver and hammer. It took seven strong hits with the hammer, but the lock eventually gave.

Magnus prised open the lid and reached inside. A book wrapped in a buckskin loincloth was all that was inside. As he tried to remove the wrapping the aged hide broke into pieces. Although the buckskin had worked in preserving the journal, the cover itself wasn't salvageable. "Sorry," he told Dane.

Dane sat on the floor beside Magnus and began to examine the loincloth. "I can't see James Bennett wearing this."

Magnus thought of the portraits he'd seen around the house. "No, neither can I." He held up the book. "Do you want me to prove to you this won't tear us apart?"

Dane reached out and ran a hand across the cracked brown leather spine. "Let me get the ham in the oven, and we'll read it together."

"You sure?"

"Yeah, I think I am."

Chapter Seven

With the ham in the oven, Dane joined Magnus in the formal living room. "I figured you'd be in the library."

Magnus shook his head and flipped the blanket that covered him back in invitation. "I wasn't sure if the fireplace in there was in working order, but since I could tell this one had been used recently I decided to do it in here. It's okay, isn't it?"

Dane joined Magnus on the sofa. "Did you read any of it yet?"

Looking guilty, Magnus nodded. "Sorry, I couldn't help myself."

Actually, Dane was glad Magnus had previewed the journal. "Good or bad?"

"Depends on your point-of-view, I guess." Magnus opened the book. "I'll read you the beginning, and you can decide for yourself if you'd like to hear more. Deal?"

"Deal." Dane turned to stretch out on the sofa and leant back against Magnus' side.

"Tell me if you want me to stop," Magnus said before he began.

December 1840

What you are about to read may shock and dishearten you, but, nonetheless, the following is a true account of what happened on Barrett Plantation in the years leading up to November 1840. It began with idealistic ideas and ended with the deaths of twenty-seven men, twenty-six women, and fourteen children.

Magnus stopped reading and kissed Dane on top of the head. "You want me to go on?"

"Hang on," Dane managed to say around the lump of emotion in his throat. Although he needed to know what had happened, the account in James' point of view was too hard to handle. "Have you read more?"

"Yeah. It's not very long, thirty-two pages," Magnus answered.

"Can you give me a summary? I think that would be easier to hear."

"I can do that, but you really should read it at some point. I may be able to get the point across, but the emotions James wrote are incredible."

"Maybe someday," Dane agreed.

Magnus closed the journal and stood. "Lay with me by the fire," he said, pulling Dane to his feet.

Dane tossed a few of the needlepoint pillows onto the floor and stretched out between Magnus and the fire. He rolled to his side to stare at the fire as Magnus began to recount James' story.

"James met a young Chitimacha brave he refers to only as his Beloved when he was barely sixteen. James knew his father wouldn't approve of the unnatural feelings he had for the brave so he ran away from home to live with his Beloved and his tribe of eighteen men, women and children. At the time, war and disease had wiped out most of the Chitimacha people, but they still held control of several small parcels of land, this island being one of them.

"When the Chitimacha chief learned of the Indian Removal Act, he knew he must do something or see the decimation of more Native tribes, including his own. Although there were other Native American tribes in the immediate area, the chief sought out the five biggest tribal leaders."

"Choctaw, Creek, Seminole, Cherokee and Chippawa," Dane added, thinking aloud.

"Yes. The chief knew soldiers would eventually find the island, so he gave it to James Bennett, the only white man he trusted. James registered the parcel of land with the government and legally became the owner.

"The next order of business was to invite warriors from the five tribes to hide on the island in exchange for protection for the Chitimacha tribe. They all agreed except the local Choctaw, whose chief felt it was too dangerous to go against the government. However, the Choctaw chief agreed to hold the information secret from the white man.

"In the spring of 1836, the warriors began to move on to the island. The first few months didn't go well, and James began to worry that there would never again be harmony on the island. Fortunately, things began to settle down and eventually peace was restored.

"Several years later, James' grandfather died and he inherited a sizeable chunk of money. James knew it was only a matter of time before the government started searching the bayous for Native Americans who were not complying with the Indian Removal Act. He felt the island needed a white man's appearance if they were going to successfully hide their Native population."

Magnus stopped talking and kissed Dane's neck. "For the next two years, the warriors and their growing families lived on the strip of land across the creek while local craftsmen worked day and night building Bennett House for James and his Beloved."

Dane tilted his head back, giving Magnus a better view of his ever-present hickey. "Fallon will be pleased to learn he wasn't the first gay man in our family." He knew it was an odd comment, but the knowledge that his family had a long history of homosexuality brought Dane comfort.

Magnus chuckled. "Yes, I suppose it will."

"So what happened in November of 1840?" Dane asked.

"Well, once Bennett House was completed and the Native population was back on the island, James was sent to Oklahoma with the necklace I showed you. It was the chief's way of showing the Choctaw that his dream had come to fruition. James delivered the necklace and carried back the Choctaw chief's written account of his people's journey to Oklahoma."

Magnus took a deep breath and pulled Dane even closer. "Are you sure you want to hear this?"

"I'm sure."

"James was gone for several weeks. By the time he returned to the island, he found it empty."

"What do you mean 'empty'?" Dane asked. "Where'd they go?"

Magnus rested his chin on Dane's shoulder, putting them cheek to cheek. "At the time, James didn't know, so he began to ask questions in New Iberia. Just as James had feared would eventually happen, soldiers had found the island. Unfortunately, the home that

James had built had worked against him instead of in his favour. The soldiers knew a white man had commissioned the home, yet James was nowhere to be found. They believed the Native Americans had killed the landowner and taken up residence on the island. There was a stand-off between the soldiers and the Native Americans. Evidently, many lives were lost on both sides. The few tribal members who survived were taken away and never heard from again."

"And what of James' Beloved?" Dane asked, although he already knew the answer.

"James found the burned bodies in a pit. He had no way of knowing if his Beloved was among them or not. He went as far as petitioning Andrew Jackson himself, trying to find out what had happened to the survivors. Unfortunately, his pleas were ignored."

"So where are the bodies?" Dane asked.

Magnus sighed. "By the end of the journal, it was quite evident James had gone mad with grief."

"What're you trying to tell me?"

"James believed the only way to protect in death what he couldn't protect in life was to wipe away all traces of them. He filled the pit with everything the Natives had owned and burned the bodies again until there was nothing but odd bones and ash. He then mixed the ash into the cement he used to build the mausoleum. What didn't burn completely, he gathered and put in the burial chamber for his Beloved."

"And that's it? Then he just went on to marry a woman and produce heirs?" Dane asked.

"Not quite. Yes, we know he went on to marry and have sons, but let me read you his last entry." Magnus reached behind him and picked up the journal.

June 1841.

After months of petitioning Washington for answers, I have decided the government must pay for the lives they have taken. I no longer care what my government dictates. I will fight them at every opportunity by offering my plantation as a means to circumvent government rules and regulations. I will have my revenge, and I will carry it out with a smile on my face.

James D Bennett.

"I guess that's why he started using the island to smuggle goods," Dane surmised. His thoughts swung to the mausoleum. "The plaque on the statue makes a lot of sense to me now." *The loss of one's soul forever changes the beauty of the landscape.* "I would imagine he was torn between leaving the island and never looking back and the desire to be close to the people he loved."

Magnus handed the journal to Dane. "Like I said before, I'd like you to read it for yourself once you feel up to it."

The story of James touched and angered Dane. It was no longer a matter of being ashamed of his fourth great-grandfather, like he'd originally feared. The illegal means James had used to amass his fortune didn't even bother him. What continued to stick with him was the anger it might cause in the Native American community. "I'd like to share the story with my mom and uncle."

Magnus nodded.

"And I'm going to need a good stonemason to come and repair the statue in the cemetery," he confessed.

Magnus narrowed his eyes. "Is that where the box came from?"

Dane nodded. "But the statue itself was still standing when I left. I just knocked a hole in the base. I also found the etched rock we've been looking for.

I'm not sure why James hid it in the base. Maybe he had second thoughts after the portrait was painted."

"And this?" Magnus brushed the cut on Dane's cheek with his thumb.

"Yeah."

Magnus kissed Dane's cheek. "We'll need to talk about what's next."

"I know."

"The detailed accounts in that journal are amazing. I'm sure the tribes involved would love to know their ancestors tried to form a unified group," Magnus reasoned.

"Maybe, but right now this island is something many of them are proud of. Do you think they'll feel the same way about it if they find out their people were massacred here?"

"I don't know, but I don't think that's our decision to make. We study, discover and report the findings. That's the job. You can't let your personal feelings cloud your judgement; it's not in the job description."

Dane sat up. "I'd better check the ham." He left the living room with the journal tucked safely against him.

* * * *

After a fantastic dinner, Magnus cleaned the kitchen while Dane phoned his family. He pulled the plug and drained the water from the sink before turning out the light. On his way upstairs, he stopped to take a look out of the front window.

Dane was still pacing the wide front porch, phone to his ear. Magnus knew in his heart that Dane would make the right decision. The journal, the hidden pages found within the library books and the mausoleum itself deserved their rightful place in Native American history. Dane span around and caught Magnus watching.

Oops. Magnus let the drape fall back into place and headed upstairs. When he passed Dane's room, he caught sight of a small wrapped package on the end of Dane's bed. *Shit. Christmas.* Buying a gift for Dane had never entered his mind before leaving Idaho. Now they'd grown closer, Magnus wished there was a department store down the street.

Fuck. Fuck. Fuck. He'd look like a real bastard if he didn't have something to give Dane, but what the hell could he come up with in the next thirty minutes? He tried to remember the last time he'd actually given someone a gift. Although he'd always been close to the Demakis brothers, he'd never gone as far as buying them gifts.

Magnus pulled out his phone and called Alec. Surely, his best friend had already shopped for his partner Max by now.

"Hey, stranger," Alec greeted.

"I've got a problem," Magnus said in return.

"More than one, but that's beside the point. How're you doing?"

"I didn't get a Christmas present for Dane," he confessed.

"You're kidding me? What the hell were you thinking? You knew the two of you were going to be down there over Christmas."

"Yeah, but I didn't know for sure things would get...intimate. Now I'm standing here staring at a gift with my name on it, and I've got nothing."

"The fact that you fucked him shouldn't have anything to do with it. You don't spend Christmas with someone without giving them a present."

"Okay, point taken. Now tell me what to do."

"Well, it's not like you can go out and buy something, so you'll have to improvise. Do something romantic. Max really goes nuts for that stuff."

Magnus chuckled. "I don't know a thing about being romantic. You'll have to give me more than that."

"I don't know, have a midnight picnic all set up under the Christmas tree or something."

"We don't have a tree," Magnus replied.

"Well there you go. Get a tree, decorate it with anything you can find then set up a picnic."

"Where the hell am I going to find a Christmas tree?"

"Improvise. As much as I'd like to talk to you all night, I need to go. We just got home from Luc and Justin's party and Max stole the mistletoe. He said something about making me a belt with it."

Magnus grinned. Alec had become a different man since he'd fallen for Max Henley. Something Magnus was beginning to understand. "Have a good time. I'll talk to you next week."

Magnus hung up and shoved the phone into his pocket. *A tree.* He stared out of the window. *Nope, no Christmas trees.* Maybe he should forget Alec's corny suggestion and just apologise for not having a present.

Unfortunately, he knew he'd probably be more comfortable chopping down a tree than apologising. "Guess the decision's been made," he said as he walked out of the room.

* * * *

After a lengthy phone conversation with his mom and uncle, Dane retreated to Magnus' bed with the journal. Magnus had blown past him on the stairs earlier, telling Dane not to wait up. Dane would have worried had it not been for the quick but tender kiss Magnus had given him.

After such an emotional day, Dane couldn't concentrate on the journal. Instead he set it on the bedside table and turned on the TV. At some point during an episode of *Will & Grace*, he fell asleep.

Warm lips kissing him woke him. "Hey," he mumbled. "What time is it?"

"Three o'clock. It's officially Christmas morning," Magnus announced.

Dane wrapped his arms around Magnus and tried to pull him down beside him. "Snuggle with me."

"Definitely, but could we do it downstairs? I have a surprise for you," Magnus said.

Dane yawned and rubbed his eyes. He didn't feel like moving, but it was obvious Magnus was excited about something. When he saw Magnus pocket a strip of condoms and grab the bottle of lube, Dane sat up. It was then he noticed the state of Magnus' clothes. "What've you been doing?"

"Well, if you get up, I'll show you." Magnus handed Dane a pair of sweatpants.

After putting on the pants, Dane was pulled to his feet and into Magnus' arms. He noticed a piece of white fuzz and picked it off Magnus' shirt. "What's this?"

Magnus glanced at the fluff. "Piece of my sock. Don't worry, it's part of your Christmas present."

"You're giving me socks for Christmas?" Dane asked as Magnus led him downstairs.

"Have you always been this inquisitive with your Christmas presents?"

Dane looked up at Magnus. "No. I used to find my gifts before they were wrapped, so come Christmas morning I already knew what I was getting." He remembered the present he'd bought Magnus. "Oh, I've got one for you, too."

When Dane turned to start back up the stairs, Magnus stopped him. "Later. Mine can't wait much longer."

Magnus stopped in front of the library door. He cleared his throat, looking incredibly uncomfortable all of a sudden.

"What's going on?" Dane asked.

"I'm not used to buying gifts for people, but I wanted to do something special. I hope you like it." Magnus opened the door and stepped back.

The first thing Dane noticed was the bookshelves. Every book had been put back. No wonder Magnus had been away for hours. His gaze scanned the room and landed on a small sapling, decorated with strips of foil and white and blue fuzz. Dane's heart melted. "You got me a tree?"

"Uh, yeah. I tried to be careful, so hopefully I didn't damage any of the roots. I'll replant it later."

Dane crossed the library and stared at the small tree, barely bigger than a sapling. He tried to imagine Magnus' big hands cutting the delicate foil into stars. Christmas in the Jefferson household had always been an elaborate affair. His parents enjoyed giving holiday parties, so more often than not the home was decorated by paid professionals. Nothing he had they'd paid for held a candle to the tree in front of him. "It's the most beautiful thing I've ever seen."

Magnus visibly relaxed. "I made breakfast, too," he said, pointing towards the small table in the corner of the room. "Originally, the plan was to have a picnic beside the tree, but I was worried you'd think that was stupid."

Dane shook his head. "Not stupid at all." He walked over to the sofa and grabbed the throw blanket before spreading it out beside the tree. "Help me move the food."

They transferred the plates of pancakes, juice, carafe of coffee and syrup to the blanket. As Dane sat cross-legged on the floor to enjoy his breakfast, he couldn't take his eyes off the tree. "I've never had someone make me a gift before."

"Sorry," Magnus mumbled. "I didn't know what else to do."

Dane tore his gaze away from the tree. "I love it." He shook his head, wishing he could find the words to explain how the gift made him feel. "I've always taken Christmas presents for granted. Don't get me wrong, I've spent years enjoying the stuff Mom and Dad gave me, but I never felt the gifts meant more than what they were." Dane motioned to the tree. "This is so much better than anything else you could've given me."

Magnus looked away first. He concentrated on cutting his pancakes and smothering them with syrup. "You'd better eat before they get any colder than they already are."

Dane didn't have the heart to tell Magnus he'd never really cared for pancakes. He took his first bite and smiled. "They're delicious, but there's no way I'll be able to eat all these." After finishing one of the pancakes, he set his plate down and picked up his juice. "So where'd you get the tree?"

"Across the creek," Magnus said around a mouthful of food.

Dane moved his plate to the side and leaned across the blanket to swipe a drop of syrup off Magnus' chin.

"Mmm, maybe I'll just pour syrup all over you and forget the pancakes."

Magnus chuckled. "I've got too much hair for that."

Dane alternated between watching Magnus eat and gazing at the tree. He wondered if the heartfelt gesture meant Magnus had changed his mind about a long-term relationship. Dane began to daydream about a future with Magnus. What kind of tree would they have next year?

"So I didn't get a chance to ask, what'd Evelyn and Fallon say about the journal?" Magnus asked, breaking through Dane's dream.

"I think they feel a lot like I do. Of course, Fallon was upset that James never knew for sure what happened to his Beloved, but they were both happy we found what we did." Dane had resigned himself to the fact that it was Magnus' decision as to what would be done with the information.

Dane waited for Magnus to swallow his last bite of pancake before reaching for the empty plate. "Have you decided what to do with the journal?"

"Usually, I'd take my findings and gather all the information into an article, but that doesn't seem like enough in this case."

Dane set the plates on the table before returning for the rest of the items. "So, what're you thinking?"

"I don't know, maybe a book." With the blanket cleared, Magnus stretched out on his back.

The thought of a book alarmed Dane. He joined Magnus on the blanket. "In order to have enough material for a book, you'd have to go into detail about James' relationship with his Beloved."

"Yeah," Magnus agreed. He narrowed his eyes. "Are you worried about that information getting out and ruining the family name?"

"What?" Dane couldn't believe Magnus would think such a thing. "No! It just bothers me that something so personal will be laid out for every bigoted sonofabitch to criticise."

Magnus pulled Dane down into his arms. "You're taking this too personally."

"How can I not? You have no idea how much time I've spent on this island, yet I never felt anything for the man who built this house. In the last two weeks, I've grown to care about James. It might sound stupid, but my heart broke for him when I found out what he'd gone through. It has nothing to do with the fact we're related. I just don't understand how you or anyone could ever consider profiting from his pain."

Dane pulled out of Magnus' arms and got to his feet. The bewildered expression on Magnus' face said it all. "I need to use the bathroom." What he really needed was to get away from Magnus long enough to pull himself together. His chest ached as he ran from the room.

* * * *

Magnus cleaned up the breakfast dishes before going back to the library. Dane was sitting next to the tree, his eyes red and swollen. A feeling of unease kept Magnus from rushing to Dane's side. "I'm sorry," he said. "This wasn't what I had planned."

Dane shook his head. "Don't apologise. I'm the one who overreacted."

Magnus took several steps towards Dane. "I won't write the book. I've been thinking about it, and you're right. I can give the facts of what happened here without bringing the relationship between James and his Beloved into it."

Dane got to his feet. "You would really do that?"

Magnus crossed the distance between them until he stood toe to toe with Dane. "I figured something out while I was cutting out all those damn stars."

"What was that?" Dane asked.

"I think I love you," Magnus confessed.

"You think?"

Magnus shrugged. "I've never been in love before, but when I read the journal I knew exactly how James felt. It confused me because I couldn't figure out how I could feel what he was going through." He gestured to the tree. "But it finally dawned on me how I knew when I was making the tree decorations. I'm in love."

Dane reached out first. He placed his palms on Magnus' chest and looked up at him. "I love you, too."

The wall around Magnus' heart crumbled. He wrapped his arms around Dane and kissed him. The warmth of Dane's mouth tasted sweet and it had nothing to do with the syrup. Suddenly he couldn't get close enough. He lowered them to the blanket without breaking the kiss and began to strip Dane of his sweatpants.

Magnus ran his hands down Dane's chest to wrap around the length of his hard cock. "You feel good," Magnus said, breaking the kiss.

Dane pulled Magnus' dirty T-shirt over his head. He buried his fingers in the thick black hair covering Magnus' chest and moaned. "So do you."

Magnus was forced to pull away long enough to get out of his jeans and underwear, but the momentary break was worth it when he covered Dane's naked body with his own. He'd been in the same position dozens of times over the previous two weeks, so why did it feel so different?

Dane pushed against Magnus' chest until Magnus rolled off him. "Too heavy?" Magnus asked.

"Too hard to touch you," Dane explained, moving to lie on his side. He draped his leg over Magnus' hip and reached for the condoms in Magnus' discarded jeans. "You still have that lube handy?"

Magnus glanced around and found the small bottle next to the galvanised bucket the tree's root ball rested in. "Got it." He popped the top and applied lubricant to his fingers. "I should probably take my time," he said as he circled Dane's hole with his middle finger. "I've fucked, but this is my first time making love, and I don't think I can wait." He pressed inside and began to stretch Dane's hole, quickly adding a second finger.

"Making love has nothing to do with the time it takes. It's about the feelings involved. Give me your heart and you can have everything I own." Dane tore open a condom wrapper and rolled the protection down Magnus' shaft.

Magnus withdrew his fingers and replaced them with the head of his cock. He eased past the outer ring of muscles until he buried his cock as deep as it would go. "More," he groaned, rolling them until he lay on top of Dane. He wished he was comfortable sharing his feelings, but he'd never done it before. As he began a slow rhythm in and out of Dane's body, he searched for the right thing to say. The moment meant too much to him to screw it up by saying something stupid. "I love you," he said, deciding simple was better.

Dane hitched his legs higher on Magnus' back. "I doubt I'll ever get tired of hearing that."

Magnus hoped that was the case. He moved in for another deep kiss as he wrapped a hand around Dane's cock. Magnus worked Dane's cock from base to tip, taking time to fondle his balls occasionally, as he continued to pound in and out of him.

Shame filled him when he allowed himself to lose control. His climax ripped through his body before he could stop it. Never, in all the years he'd been fucking, had he allowed himself release before a partner.

As he struggled to catch his breath, it took all of Magnus' strength to continue to jack Dane's cock. He pulled out and quickly scooted down to swallow Dane's cock. Magnus used his tongue to try and tickle the sensitive area just under the head like Dane had done to him. To his astonishment, the trick worked just as well on Dane as it had on himself.

"Oh, fuck!" Dane screamed as he came.

It happened so fast, Magnus wasn't prepared. He tried to swallow, but couldn't figure out how to do it and not clamp down on Dane's cock. With no other choice, Magnus removed the cock from his mouth and tried to concentrate on catching the seed on his tongue as it shot in short bursts.

Magnus knew his performance was pitiful. How would he be able to look Dane in the eyes after something like that? The moment Dane finished coming, Magnus pulled away and got to his feet. He removed the condom on his way to the downstairs restroom.

After disposing of the condom, Magnus wet a washcloth with warm water. He caught his own gaze in the mirror and shook his head. "You really fucked up," he admonished himself.

He spent several moments getting himself together, finally deciding to just apologise for the disastrous performance. The first thing he noticed upon re-entering the library was Dane biting his thumbnail, a clear sign something was wrong.

Magnus sat down, ready to face the music. "Here." He offered the washcloth to Dane.

Dane lowered his thumb and took the cloth. "You're not going to tell me things are over between us when we leave here, are you?"

For years, his self-imposed rules had allowed Magnus to guard his heart. The fear that he'd be hurt suddenly threatened to overwhelm him. He knew his heart wouldn't survive another break. "I wasn't planning on it. Why? Is that what you want?"

"No." Dane cupped Magnus' cheek. "God, no. Just...you know, the way you left like that..."

"I left because I was embarrassed."

"Why?" Dane asked.

"I lost control. It should've never happened like that."

"You mean because you came first? It's not a contest." Dane shrugged. "Actually, I was going to say the opposite. It made me feel good to see you lose some of that control you're so proud of. Made me feel special."

"You are special." Magnus took the washcloth back and began to clean Dane. "I just hope I can make you happy."

"You already have. You mean everything to me." Dane brushed a kiss across Magnus' lips. "You're my beloved."

Magnus closed his eyes to hide the sting of tears. He knew in that moment what he meant to Dane and he felt the same way. "As you are mine," he whispered.

* * * *

Dane woke several hours later with a crick in his neck. He untangled himself from Magnus and scooted out from under the blanket. After Magnus' special gift, his seemed stupid in comparison, but he had nothing else to give.

He ran up to the bedroom and retrieved the small wrapped box from the foot of his bed before returning to the library. Rejoining Magnus under the blanket, Dane propped his head on his hand and watched Magnus sleep. He'd been so tired earlier he hadn't taken the time to realise what a future with Magnus could mean. The job as Magnus' teaching assistant wasn't that big of a deal. He could easily afford to quit and he'd only taken the position in the first place so he could be closer to Magnus.

"You're thinking too hard," Magnus mumbled, his voice deep and raspy.

"Just wondering what'll happen when we go back home," Dane admitted.

"Whatever we want to happen. Why? You getting nervous?"

"No. More excited than anything. I don't have you for any classes next semester, so that should help. And I'll help you find another TA." Dane tried to think of another graduate student who could easily slide into the job. "A woman," he added.

Magnus grinned. "Don't you trust me?"

"Oh, I trust you, but I'm not the only student with a crush on you." Dane sat up and set the small gift on Magnus' chest. "It's not much, but I saw it last summer when I went to Italy with my parents and thought of you."

Magnus looked surprised. "You bought it last summer?"

"Yeah." Dane shrugged. "I didn't even know at the time whether I'd have the guts to give it to you, but I got it anyway."

Magnus carefully unwrapped the present. He took the lid off the box and separated the white tissue paper to reveal the leather journal. "It's gorgeous," he said, running his fingertips over the sunburst embossed into the leather.

"I don't know if you journal or not, but you're such a secretive person, I figured you might," Dane explained.

"I don't." Magnus flipped through the blank pages. "I never had anything but pain to write about. Since I lived it, I never saw the point of recording it on paper." He set the box aside and pulled Dane into his lap. "I think I'd enjoy it now though. If you don't mind, I'd like to record what's happened since we've been here."

"You mean all the stuff with James?" Dane asked.

"Nope. I discovered something far more important on this trip. I learned that sometimes forgetting the past is the only way to forge a future. It was a good lesson to learn, and one only you could have taught me.

Epilogue

Locked in a heated kiss with Magnus, Dane jumped when someone knocked on the car window behind him.

"You coming in, or do you plan to make out in my driveway all night?" Demitri asked.

"We'll be in once the party starts," Magnus yelled back.

Demitri laughed and walked back into the house. "Where were we?" Magnus asked, pulling Dane into his arms once more.

"Your friends sure do have a lot of parties." Dane liked Magnus' friends. They had all been incredibly nice to him since Magnus had introduced him as his boyfriend on New Year's Eve, but Dane still hadn't been able to overcome his social anxiety when the entire group got together.

Magnus licked the fresh bruise on Dane's neck. "I know, but it's tradition that we watch the Super Bowl together." He scraped his teeth across the hickey.

"I'm glad I brought a book," he mumbled.

A car door slamming caught Dane's attention. "Oh, shit."

Magnus sat up and looked around. "What's he doing here?"

"Good question." Dane gave Magnus a quick kiss before getting out of the car. "Uncle Fallon?" he asked.

Fallon stopped and spread his arms. "What, no hug?"

As much as Dane loved his uncle, he didn't trust him. He gave Fallon a hug before stepping back. "Are you here to cause problems for Tony and Daniel?"

"I told you I was working on a business deal with Tony. Actually, I was hoping you'd let me stay at your place while I'm in town."

Dane glanced over his shoulder. Magnus stood on the front step with his arms crossed. No matter how many times Dane had tried, Magnus and Fallon still didn't get along. "You said you were coming at the end of February. It's only the fifth, so why so early?"

"I was bored, so I thought I'd head on up. If it's a problem, I can get a hotel."

Dane stared at his uncle. "Promise me you're not going to try and come between Tony and Daniel."

"Hey, if their relationship is as strong as you say it is, there won't be enough room for me to come between them, right?" Fallon reached out and mussed Dane's hair. "You worry too much, Monkey."

Magnus cleared his throat. "You ready?" he asked Dane.

"Yeah." Dane turned away from his uncle and joined Magnus.

Fallon met them at the front porch and Magnus pulled Dane to the side. "Go ahead," he told Fallon.

Fallon smirked and went inside the house.

"Be nice," Dane whispered in Magnus' ear.

"I'm nothing but nice. He's the one with the chip on his shoulder," Magnus grumbled.

"He still believes you're going to write a book about James Bennett."

"How can I do that when we sealed the journal back in the base of the statue? I tell you what; if he honestly thinks I'm a man who would go against my word we're going to have serious problems."

Dane knew deep down the two men were simply too much alike. If they both dropped their defences long enough to actually get to know each other, they would probably become the best of friends. Unfortunately, Dane didn't see that happening any time soon.

"I'll talk to him," Dane promised. "I just don't want whatever's going on with the two of you to come between us."

Magnus looked surprised by the comment. "Why would it?" He pulled Dane against him. "I love you. That's not going to change. You're the first good thing to ever come into my life. I'm not fool enough to let anything get in the way of that."

"Good." Dane wrapped his arms around Magnus' neck and pulled him down for a kiss. "I love you, too, but promise me we can skip the annual Valentine's Day party?"

"Who said there was a Valentine's Day party?"

"Is there?" Dane asked.

"Yeah, but I've never been to it. Of course, I've never had a Valentine to share the occasion with."

"Me neither; and I plan to share it with the man I love and no one else."

Magnus squeezed Dane's ass. "I can live with that."

* * * *

"I'm gonna grab another beer, do you want anything?" Magnus asked with a kiss to Dane's neck. He was glad Daniel had asked Dane to play a game. Watching football obviously didn't hold Dane's attention. At least this way, Magnus could still enjoy the game while Dane had fun with his friends.

Dane glanced up from the Scrabble board. "I'm fine."

Magnus stole another quick kiss before leaving Dane, Bobby and Daniel to continue their game. He walked into the kitchen and started to rinse his empty beer bottle. What he saw on the deck floored him. Fallon was tongue fucking Becket Chandler. "What the hell?"

Locky, the new activity director at BK House, came into the room and opened the fridge. "What's going on?"

"Nothing." Magnus shut off the water and tossed the bottle into the recycle bin. "I just can't believe how fast Dane's uncle works."

Locky handed Magnus a beer before glancing out of the window. "Oh, fuck! That guy's gotta be twice Becket's age." He slammed his beer onto the counter, causing the beer to erupt from the bottle before throwing open the back door.

Magnus managed to get the beer into the sink before the foam made too big a mess. He found a dishcloth and began to clean up the foam, keeping one eye on the action out of the window. He wasn't sure what the story was, but Locky seemed mad as hell at Fallon and Becket.

When Locky took a swing at Fallon, Magnus knew he couldn't stand by and do nothing. He dropped the dishcloth in the sink and opened the back door just in time to see Fallon charge Locky in retaliation.

"Enough!" Magnus yelled, trying to get between the two men.

"He started it," Fallon said, pushing against Magnus' hold.

"You started it by coming on to a kid half your fucking age," Locky shot back.

Magnus happened to catch the satisfied grin on Becket's face before the younger man walked out of the side gate. *Mmm-hmm.* Magnus had a good idea about what was going on. He shook Fallon to get his attention. "Get hold of yourself."

Magnus glanced over his shoulder at Locky. "You'd better go make sure Becket's okay."

Locky tore his angered gaze from Fallon to look around the deck. "Where'd he go?"

"Side gate," Magnus answered.

Before Locky left, he pointed his finger at Fallon. "You keep your fucking hands off the kids in my dorm."

Once he was left alone with Fallon, Magnus released him. "I think you were just used," he informed Fallon.

Fallon touched his kiss-swollen lips. "Yeah, well, if the guy wants to use me, who am I to complain?"

"Do yourself a favour and stay away from him." Magnus turned to go back into the house.

"You think I'm afraid of you?" Fallon asked Magnus' retreating back.

With his hand on the doorknob, Magnus turned to stare at Fallon. Although he'd love to prove to him why he should be afraid, his first thought was for Dane. "Look, I'm not the bad guy here. There's obviously something going on between those two. I'm just trying to save you the trouble."

Fallon broke eye contact to look towards the side gate. "Maybe I don't need you to save me. Anything's better than nothing."

There was something in the way Fallon said it that didn't match up with the man Magnus believed Fallon to be. "No, take it from me. You can spend your life fucking a different guy every night, but all it takes is one time in the arms of a man you love to make you realise you've never truly known what it means to be with someone."

Fallon winced. "That's my nephew you're talking about."

"Yeah, but he's also the best thing that's ever happened to me. You and I don't have to like each other, but I don't plan on going anywhere, so maybe it would be easier if we learned to get along."

Fallon straightened his heavy wool topcoat. "If you had a son, would you approve of him dating someone like you?"

Magnus had no doubt Fallon thought he was after Dane's money, but nothing could be further from the truth. For years, Magnus had exerted control over people so they didn't get close enough to see his damaged heart. All that had changed when he'd opened himself to Dane's love. Dane made him feel like the luckiest man in the world. Even after learning everything there was to know about Magnus' childhood, Dane still believed he was worthy.

Looking at the man in the two-thousand-dollar coat, Magnus nodded. "Yeah, I would. Dane believes in me. Maybe that's all I ever needed. Maybe that's all anybody needs."

Magnus left Fallon on the porch and walked back into the dining room. "How's the game?" he asked Dane.

"Daniel's trying to skunk us, but I'm not giving up," Dane mumbled, concentrating on his tiles. He glanced up at Magnus. "Thanks, you must be my good luck charm." He gathered his letters and began laying them out on the board. B-E-L-O-V-E-D

"Perfect," Magnus said, kissing the top of Dane's head.

About the Author

An avid reader for years, one day Carol Lynne decided to write her own brand of erotic romance. Carol juggles between being a full-time mother and a full-time writer. These days, you can usually find Carol either cleaning jelly out of the carpet or nestled in her favourite chair writing steamy love scenes.

Carol Lynne loves to hear from readers.

You can find her contact information, website details and author profile page at http://www.total-e-bound.com.

Total-E-Bound Publishing

www.total-e-bound.com

Take a look at our exciting range of literagasmic™
erotic romance titles and discover pure quality
at Total-E-Bound.